S. Fuller

Another Heaven, Another Earth

BY THE SAME AUTHOR

The Delikon

The Lost Star

The Rains of Eridan

Return to Earth

This Time of Darkness

H. M. HOOVER

Another Heaven, Another Earth

THE VIKING PRESS   NEW YORK

First Edition
Copyright © H. M. Hoover, 1981
All rights reserved
First published in 1981 by The Viking Press
625 Madison Avenue, New York, N.Y. 10022
Published simultaneously in Canada by Penguin Books Canada Limited
Printed in U.S.A.
1 2 3 4 5 85 84 83 82 81

Library of Congress Cataloging in Publication Data
Hoover, H. M.   Another heaven, another Earth.
Summary: After being lost for several hundred years,
a space colony is rediscovered by an exploratory
expedition from Earth whose technology threatens to
destroy the colony's painfully constructed civilization.
[1. Science fiction]   I. Title.
PZ7.H7705An   [Fic]   81–2622   ISBN 0–670–12883–x   AACR2

FOR ROSIE

Another Heaven, Another Earth

P R O L O G U E

THE VILLAGE STOOD WELL BACK FROM THE SEA, SECURE IN A peaceful valley. Fields ended in forest long before the eastern mountains. A dirt road led south across the fields and up a wooded hill to what looked like a ruined fort. The tallest structure inside the crumbling walls looked north, across valley and village, to another hill at the edge of the sea. There, looming up out of the trees, stood an enormous cube of metal, rusty orange with age, alien to all its surroundings.

The cube rested on a circular base and had one slanting wall, shiny and segmented like a monstrous insect's eye. Like the fortlike structure, the cube was a relic of the misty past.

Sometimes in the night the cube turned on its base and starlight glinted off the eye. Flashes of refracted light would frighten birds and lizards nesting on the offshore rocks, and they would startle and cry out and fly in aimless circles. Disturbed by the cries, the villagers would stir in their sleep and whisper prayers against old powers.

They could not understand how a thing so large could turn, quickly and silently, despite its rusted bulk. They believed that something had been worshiped there, that the cube had been a temple—although to what or whom was as much a mystery as the source of its mobility. The villagers kept away from it and had for as long as could be remembered.

For three nights now the thing had turned as if the eye restlessly sought something. Worse, from inside its walls, voices began to whisper and, as the hours passed, to speak in tones that echoed down the valley. The villagers were terrified. Nothing human could be alive inside that thing. When two days more had passed, the village council decided to burn the spirits out, to heat the cube by fire and kill the force inside.

If any villager disagreed, he kept his doubts to himself and helped to gather wood. But the people from the old compound protested the destruction of the last intact building from their ancient past.

The council ignored them; the people in the compound had always held themselves too dear, proud of being descendants of those long-ago Builders of that menace on the hill. The family name of Mitchell could still be seen, cut in block letters on one corner of the cube. The villagers understood when Gareth Mitchell called them "ignorant and superstitious"—she was only protecting her own—and they went on hauling wood.

CHAPTER 1

AT SUNSET THEY LIT THE BONFIRES BUILT AROUND THE CUBE. The sea wind caught the flames and fanned them upward through the brush. The fires were well laid; soon each cone-shape pyre was torching up against the walls. The villagers stepped back and watched, ready with more fuel. The cube was still and silent, as it had been since dawn.

Gareth Mitchell stood alone on the cliff path to the beach. She knew she wasn't welcome here. No one had waved or said hello—she thought they were ashamed to. It was easier for them to pretend she wasn't there. She'd known them all her life, been their only medic for a year. They had come to her with their wounds and diseases and some of their sorrows. And now they wouldn't look her way, wouldn't meet her glance.

A gray flint lizard elbowed its way out of the grass and down into the path. It paused to smell her boot with a flick of its dark tongue, then journeyed onward, its delicate splayed fingers leaving handprints on the sand. She watched it go and envied it, so perfect in design, so safe inside its armor-plated solitude, so seemingly content to be exactly what and where it was. A cold breeze blew and she pulled her leather cape close.

The smoke diminished as the flames grew more intense. Heat waves rose to distort the prisms of the eye. Where the square overhung the circular base, naphtha was added to the fire to take advantage of this vulnerability. She could see the metal corners beginning to glow red. That upset her, and she turned and faced the sea.

The sun was gone. A line of dark blue clouds rimmed the horizon. Just above the clouds an early star winked brightly. She stared at it, distracted by the fires' crackling, and slowly realized the star was moving toward her. It came directly overhead, in a line across the sky, passed behind high clouds that dimmed it, and then reappeared to drop behind the mountains.

A shout went up on the hillside. The cube was turning. The tallest timbers supporting the pyres had been pressed against the walls. These were being shoved, screeching and protesting and thrown aside in showers of sparks and smoke. Burning logs and embers rolled. People were running and yelling. The cube swung around until the eye faced the mountains, until all the fires had been scattered. It had shrugged off its attackers.

Gareth began to laugh with relief. They had won, she and that beautiful old thing! Had she been asked, she couldn't have explained why she loved it, but she did. She didn't even know what it was, and the mystery was part of its charm. It had no known purpose, no use—it simply was. Solid and forever. She knew it wasn't a temple, but for her it was, and when she walked there, the very air felt good, as if once, long ago, something wonderful had happened here and joy had permeated the hill and trees.

When she was little, she used to press her hands against the base, and it seemed to her then that she could feel it living. That vibrancy was gone, lost with childhood, but when she was troubled, she still came here to let the spirit of the place ease her soul.

The cube began to turn again, back toward the sea. She'd never been this close before when it moved; when one stood beneath, looking up, the moving bulk was awesome. Light from a high pink cloud fragmented on a hundred mirrored facets and was gone. Birds on the rocks offshore broke into frightened cries as bright and scattered as the light.

Wind whipped in a sudden gust and sent sparks and ashes flying. The villagers backed away from the scattered fires. Some were slapping embers from their clothes and hair, others rubbed their eyes. Her first impulse was to ask if they needed help, and then she thought, Why bother? They don't know I'm here. She pulled her cape around her and set off down the path.

When she got home, she thought, she would light the fire, toast some bread and cheese, have some wine, and go to bed. Tomorrow she would get up early and go herb hunting, get away and forget how silly decent people could be when they were frightened by something they couldn't understand. She began a mental inventory of the drugs in short supply and the plants she'd have to gather to replace them.

There was yelling again on the hill. A breaker smashed against the rocks and drowned out another shout. The fire had spread to a thicket and beyond to dry grass on the hill. Pushed by the wind, it was licking toward a field of ripening grain. If that field caught, the next fuel would be the village.

She ran back, shrugging off her cape to use as a flail in beating out the flames. People were milling about, unsure of what to do. "Forget about the cube!" she yelled as she ran to join them. "Stop the grass fire!"

Something struck a hard glancing blow to her shoulder. She ignored it, thinking it was fire-flung debris. A rough hand reached out and grabbed her arm, spinning her around, nearly causing her to fall.

"Get out of here!" a man yelled. It was Luther Buri, the council leader. "Go home! We don't need your help!" He was in a rage and gray with ash and soot.

"What's wrong with you?" She pulled free.

"Get out!"

"Don't you see the fire? Are you crazy?"

As soon as she said it, she knew it had been the wrong thing to say since, at the moment, Luther apparently was. He swung at her, hard enough to have broken her jaw if she hadn't ducked. Two other men grabbed him by the arms then or he would have knocked her down.

"You laughed!" Luther yelled, struggling to get at her. "You saw that thing turn and you laughed! Do you know how hard we worked to build that fire? Do you know how long it took to gather that much wood? The weight of it? And you see it go to waste and laugh? God, I'd like to kill you!"

"Luther!" one of the men said, shocked. "You don't mean that."

"Yes, he does, Eugene," Gareth said, knowing it was true and frightened by the knowledge. "But I didn't laugh at you—or anyone else. I laughed because—I was relieved—because . . ." She couldn't think how to make him understand. "I wasn't laughing at you. We can talk later. Let's get the grass fire out."

"No!" Luther shouted. "I won't have you here!"

"What's going on?" Ula, Luther's wife, came running out of the smoky dusk. "Luther? Mike? What's the matter?" She eyed the men's grip on her husband, and they shyly let go.

"Nothing—" Gareth started to say.

"You laughed!" Luther yelled. "That's not nothing! You said I was crazy. You laughed at all of us. I saw you! I was watching." The three around him looked at Gareth; doubt and resentment mingled with concern in their faces. "You people in the compound think you're all so smart. You worship books and do things. You don't care about us."

"Since when is it 'us' against 'you people'?" Gareth said, beginning to get angry. "Since when do we—"

"It's always been! Always! You just pretend it's not."

"We've always worked together—"

"You've never worked the fields! None of you!" There were tears in Luther's eyes, although whether they were tears of frustration or self-pity she couldn't tell. "You're the *craftsmen*. You're the *experts*. You're right and we're wrong! When it rains you can sit indoors and make your harnesses and hammer copper pots. You don't have to muck out stables and get your leg slashed by a strider—"

"No, but I have to come sew you up then, don't I?" Gareth

snapped. "Whether it's raining or not. This whole argument is stupid! The fire's—"

"I'm not stupid!" He would have struck her then, but Ula stepped between them and deflected the blow. Ula staggered and would have fallen if Gareth hadn't caught her.

"What's the matter with him?" Gareth asked her, but Ula shook her head, pulled free, and stood erect.

"He's overtired, that's all. You'd better go home now," Ula said. "You people wanted nothing to do with tonight. You shouldn't have come over." Gareth hesitated, not wanting to leave it at this.

"Just go—please?" Ula begged.

Gareth looked from Luther's rage to Ula's pleading eyes and nodded. "Yes, I'm sorry you got hit."

Ula didn't answer, and there was something in the woman's look Gareth didn't understand; some old resentment had flared up that she'd been unaware existed. Suddenly she didn't care any more, about the fire or the fight or Ula. It was all too involved and senseless, and she was tired of them all. She bent to pick up her cape and left without another word. As she turned to go down the cliff path, she saw people coming across the field from the village, carrying shovels and wet sacks. Not everyone had gone crazy.

The tide was coming in, and waves slopped and surged around the rocks of the fishing pier. She walked fast, angry and upset, her boot heels punching holes in the damp sand. It was almost nightfall.

When she climbed the dunes, she had cooled down enough to put her cape on and think rationally again.

Luther had wanted to kill her. The question was: why? She didn't think her laughter was adequate cause—unless he interpreted it as humiliating. Setting fire to the cube had been his idea and a failure.

It was possible that he really was going crazy. He was at that age when people did. Some grew moody and suspicious, afraid of everyone; some stumbled, unsure of their muscles; and a few killed themselves when they felt the symptoms coming on. Her parents had taught her to look for the gleam of copper in the eyes, painful joints, and faces that smiled without wanting to smile. She would have to look closely at Luther's eyes, if he'd let her near, or ask Ula. Maybe he was losing his mind, but that didn't explain what sounded like old hatred, or Ula's look of resentment.

Gareth climbed the last dune and took the path through the windbreak that protected fields from sea. The silver swords had been planted here so long ago that generations of children had played among the big succulents, using their massive broad leaves as slides, or climbing up, leaf by leaf, to peer down into the hollow center. "If you fall in one you have to stay there forever," children warned each other, and until Gareth was old enough to think of being pulled out by rope, she'd had bad dreams of being trapped inside a plant.

Remembering that tonight, she smiled to herself; no child could imagine all the ways one could be trapped—ways no rope was long enough to reach.

Night had come by the time she reached the woods. The hardroad, the only stretch still left intact, felt welcome after the sand. She paused outside the compound gate for one last look across the valley. Lamps were lit in the village houses. Mist hung above the fields. So familiar a sight—why did she feel a stranger?

She went inside and tripped the balance lever on the gate. The big panel slid down smoothly. She locked it into place and leaned against its comforting security.

For want of any other explanation she had always assumed the walls and gate were built to keep out animals, but tonight she wondered. What animal here required defenses like this? The most dangerous ones were in the sea . . . except for people. She would have to ask Paul. He knew a lot of history.

Within the dark compound was an oval green where an artesian spring pumped into a fountain reservoir. Both green and reservoir were wild and overgrown. The buildings rimming the wall had fallen into ruin. Doors were gone; windows gaped open; wild things nested on the upper floors. Creeper vines were covering up the walls.

Gareth stopped for a drink at the fountain. One ornamental light still glowed beneath the water. Tiny fish scattered as she dipped her hand. Across the way was a lighted dome so old the panels had filmed into opaque amber. Margo was still working; she could hear the loom. Another light gleamed in the windows of a long, low building, part of which had fallen down. Above one window the word AIRD was embedded in frosty plastic. Only partial walls of other buildings remained, and Gareth's house, a great crumbling pile of adobe-like stuff.

A faint hissing sound made her look up. Overhead another star was falling, this one lower and much brighter. She saw only a trace of it before the trees shut off her view, but that was enough to worry her. The insects had quit singing and stayed silent for minutes, as if listening or waiting. She tried to remember what her father had told her about meteors. Did they ever hit the ground intact? And how big were they if they fell?

CHAPTER 2

ALWAYS IN THOSE FIRST FEW MINUTES WHEN THE SHUTTLE left the parent ship and accelerated to clear the gravitational pull of the larger mass, Lee was sure she had made a terrible mistake. Anticipation changed to terror. She didn't belong here; none of them did—fragile creatures set in rows in a canister shot through black space. She belonged to Earth. To be here was madness, an insane presumption, and there was no way to escape. If their canister exploded, five years would pass before anyone on Earth knew they were missing.

All she was, all she had accomplished, meant nothing in this time of desperate sanity. The fifty-odd men and women in the cabin with her were all accomplished, all experts in their fields, and all incidental.

The screen mounted in the seat ahead reflected her face, blurred by a thousand moving stars. It was not a good mirror, but it was the best she had. It reflected highlights, a ram's horn curve of eyebrows and nose, angles of chin and cheekbone. Her deep-set eyes, bright with awareness, took in and then dismissed her image as being no more real than the points of ancient light that represented stars.

As the shuttle turned, the cameras gave them a view of the *Kekule*, the parent ship receding in the distance. Three miles long, half a mile deep and wide, the starship was a tribute to the art of welding. It floated in deep space like a chunk of bizarre litter. The word "starship" evoked a far more poetic image than the real thing, Lee thought as she watched.

Around her people talked and laughed. She didn't join in, nor did they try to talk to her. Past experience had taught them she was best left alone in shuttles—unless they wanted to be snapped at. In the confinement of starships individual quirks became well-known.

The planet Xilan appeared on the screen, as green as Earth was blue. From this distance it suggested an agate ball, variegated with white, shining and untouched. It had been discovered five hundred Earth years before; there were records of several landings there, but little more than basic data survived in the corporate archives. At the time of its discovery Xilan had been considered too far from Earth to make colonization profitable, too far to plunder for mineral wealth. Technology was changing that.

Hours passed. Polar ice caps and land masses came into focus. The white became clouds and then the gleam of snow-capped mountains. A wide tapering of beige suggested that desert covered the center of one continent. Rivers veined into view. Several volcanoes plumed into the upper atmosphere.

For Leland Hamlin, biologist, all this had just one joyous message—a wide variety of life forms existed on this world, animals never seen before, each one unique and fascinating. The archives reported only non-sentient life forms here, but to her that proved nothing. Five hundred years earlier, tests of sentience had been crude, full of Earthly chauvinism, unreliable.

Born in a ring-world colony in L_5, she had grown up without ever seeing any animal but man—and she missed animals. Her father said she was a product of a more primitive era. The data banks of her first learning center had been almost exclusively devoted to zoology. At fourteen, she had qualified for a scholarship at an Earthside university.

She had gone to her home planet expecting to find the wealth of species detailed in her studies. She found instead that man had indeed inherited the Earth and had permitted only those creatures which served him to survive. The rest were extinct and had been for generations past. The child in her never quite forgave her ancestors for that crime.

The ancient zoologist Beebe had written, ". . . when the last individual of a race of living things breathes no more, another heaven and another earth must pass before such a one can come again." And so, finding Earth desolate, she searched.

It was not a quest one could go on alone, although she would have liked to. But she had learned the practical must enter into the realization of any dream, so when an employment recruiter from one of Earth's largest corporations offered her a job as a biochemist on a deep space exploration venture, she accepted.

Fifteen space years had passed since then, and five more expeditions. Study during travel time had earned her two more doctorates. Two of her trip logs had been so well written, so alive with her enthusiasm, that they sold throughout Earth's federation as popular adventure books. She had gained also in that time a devout respect for life. It was so rare a phenomenon. Entire galaxies existed without a trace of it. Billions of years passed on planets while nothing ever changed but rock.

On Xilen's night side, in the lowest and last orbit, she saw a dull red glow of surface fire and something glinting in its light—lightning-struck vegetation, or molten lava? The shuttle was too close to the surface and moving too fast for its cameras to see clearly. She glanced at nearby colleagues; none seemed to have noticed anything remarkable. The belltone signaled that they were landing.

When the cruiser *Kekule* had first entered Xilan's orbit, the engineering and supply crews had been sent out to set up camp for the research expedition. The shuttle landed on the airstrip of that base.

Pole lights shone on a small village that looked as if it had been spun of brown sugar. Native sand, converted to foam and sprayed over inflated molds, created durable, well-insulated structures, quickly and at low cost. Neat roadways curved around the trees, connecting living and working quarters.

As they came down the ramp, Lee inhaled deeply, glad to breathe a natural atmosphere again. The smells of dust, humans, and the cooling metal of the shuttle predominated, but there were foreign odors too. A spicy citrus-like scent could have been crushed grass, or the blossoms on the slender trees across the way. A stronger odor suggested tidal wrack.

"Something *stinks!*" a voice complained. Others quickly agreed. The research staff, used to the sterile air of the ship, found the natural scents offensive.

Lee, who'd been enjoying the smells, knew the irritation the griping aroused in her was out of proportion, but after years of close confinement with the same people, one lost perspective. All she wanted at the moment was the luxury of solitude. Instead, she stood in line at the field desk on the landing pad, waited for the housekeeping exec to assign her her living quarters, and listened to the complaints he was being subjected to.

A botanist refused to room with a geologist who scratched in his sleep. A mycologist had to make sure immediately that all her allergy drugs had been sent down and were properly stored. An agronomist could not stand the color of the blankets on his bed. Out of charity Lee guessed that most of the complaints were prompted by anxieties much like her own, that they were an excuse to keep people from admitting their fear of this new world. But her pragmatic side was impatient with them all.

As the crowd shifted, the harassed exec looked up, saw her there, and smiled, relieved to find a quiet face. His name was Major Singh, and in the years she'd worked with him she'd often marveled at his patience as well as his efficiency. Something about him reminded her of a large, good-natured dog, gentle because you both knew he could take your arm off if he had to.

"Dr. Hamlin!" He stood up and reached through the crowd to shake her hand.

"Good evening, Major Singh."

"It was until these prima donnas landed," the big man grumbled, then muttered something into his terminal transmitter before meeting her eyes again. "You're going to like it here, doctor. Animals up the kazoo. Too many—"

"Could you solve my problem before indulging in social chitchat?" the botanist wanted to know. "I'm ahead of her."

Major Singh ignored him. "Too many flying things for my tastes, but the flowers make up for that. Just don't do too much until you're used to the thin air. A couple of my crew got sick—"

"Hamlin, Leland Kay, senior field study officer," the transmitter interrupted. "Assigned to Number 9, Beach Row. Personal belongings have been transferred. A car has been—"

"Right!" The major interrupted the computer. "It's a good location. Nice view of the sea. Driver!" he bawled out to a scooter car that came rolling toward the group. "Take Dr. Hamlin over to her quarters."

"Just a minute."

"I was here first!"

"Why should she get special treatment?"

"Please," Lee said before an incident could happen, "I'd rather walk. I'd like the exercise."

"Oh. O.K. Sure." Major Singh glared at the gripers, feeling they had pushed her into this. "It's about half a mile down the road there." He pointed. "You can't miss it. Just keep going right."

The hubbub faded behind her as she walked. The landing area was at the top of a long slope to the ocean, the roadway to the base marked by globe lights. In the quiet she inhaled deeply and relaxed, glad to be outdoors again, to feel wind and smell trees and grass.

After looking about carefully to make sure she couldn't be seen, she tried a few experimental skips and jumps and hops, delighting in her sudden weight reduction. The gravity on Xilan was two-thirds that of Earth. That the oxygen level was also reduced was quickly made evident by the pounding of her heart. She stopped to unhook the mask on her adapter belt and breathe in deep, restoring gulps of oxygen. With clinical detachment she noted that her head was threatening to ache and decided she would not skip again unless she wore a helmet.

Somewhere in the grass a creature croaked "rupp-rupp." A more distant "rupp-rupp" answered, and she wondered if they were warning of her, a monster in their world. Something blue was running along the edge of the circle of light ahead; she hurried to catch her first glimpse of a native of Xilan.

The beep-beep horn of a scooter car made her jump. Its headlight threw her shadow yards down the road and frightened the blue thing back into the darkness.

"Want a lift?" the driver called, stopping alongside. "We'll make room."

"Hop on," the botanist invited, obviously in a forgiving mood.

Lee looked at the crowded car and shook her head. "No, thanks."

"O.K." The driver hesitated and then eased the car back into gear. "You're only halfway there," she said. "The science compound's right along the shore."

"I'll find it," Lee promised and waved them on, but as she watched the ruby taillights grow smaller in the distance, an old memory was triggered and she felt a sudden acute sense of being left behind, left out, like a child who is chosen by neither side for the game and stands forlorn on the edge of the playing field. She had been that child once, too bright, too tall, too different from other children. Sometimes she thought that was why she adapted so well to other worlds; they weren't that much different from home. But she seldom thought about it much and, recognizing the child now, she acknowledged that younger, more vulnerable self, and walked on.

C H A P T E R 3

THE LIGHTS WERE ON IN NUMBER 9, AS THEY WERE IN ALL THE windows on the row. Inside, the furnishings were spartan but adequate, with carpet and bedding all in red, the corporate color. The effect of red on beige was jolly, childlike. Her luggage was stacked in a neat pile against one wall. It looked like the same efficient room she'd lived in on the last world, and the one before that, or three worlds to come. "A house built of sand," she whispered to the quiet as she closed the door behind her.

Powdered sand filmed every flat surface in the room—the result of hasty construction. The first thing she did was to take a towel, dampen it, and proceed to dust.

"There's no point in doing that," a familiar voice said from the window. "It'll just get dirty again."

Tai Kim called herself a mineral maven, but she was more than that. Her doctorate in geology didn't explain how she could look at a landscape and tell, with almost occult accuracy, what precious metals or metallic ores, and in what quantity, were hidden beneath the surface. This gift made Dr. Kim valuable to the corporation, but it was the woman Lee appreciated. Unlike so many of the staff, there was no temperament to her. She was calm, totally dependable, and quite whole.

"Casual" was a kind word for Tai's style. Her living quarters always looked as if they'd been stirred up with a stick. Hair flared around her face like a black lion's ruff, and no comb retained all its teeth after sorting through that curly tangle. Tai could put on a spotless uniform and it instantly looked slept in. She never seemed to bother about her appearance, so long as she was clean.

If she had any vanity, it was for her hands. They were small and tapered, with oval nails—childlike hands until one saw the palms. The palms were lined and grooved and crossed with tiny squares and stars like the hands of an ancient. Once she had caught Lee staring at them and explained, "I see with them —that's why they look like that." When Lee had frowned, not understanding, Tai had laughed and changed the subject.

"Wesley Hall has a fire going on the beach," Tai announced. Although he had been her husband for some twenty years, Tai always called him by his full name. "Wesley Hall said to come tell you he's making a barbecue, that three years without the taste of woodsmoke is more than a man should have to put up with. He says you get sterile unless you eat a little dirt now and then."

Lee grinned; that sounded like Wes. A gaunt blond man with a boyish face, he was a biochemist who liked to pretend he was born into an earlier time.

"He analyzed the wood?"

"Nothing lethal," Tai assured her.

"What's he barbecuing?"

"God knows. Something he stole from the cooks."

"Oh."

"Wesley Hall wants to go home after this trip. He says he wants real meat in his old age."

"Wes isn't old."

"He will be by the time we get back to Earth. Both of us. Two hundred years have gone by back there since we were born." Tai rested her ample arms on the windowsill, stared sadly at the floor, and sighed. "We probably can't even digest real meat any more."

Lee, who had assumed Tai's sadness was inspired by thoughts of Earth time and people long since gone, and was prepared to sympathize, now fought the urge to laugh. "Your stomachs will readjust—with practice," she said quickly.

"You think so?"

"Sure. If you start out slowly and work up."

Tai's face brightened, encouraged by the idea. "You coming to the beach? It looks like a big party."

"No. Tell Wes thank you, but I want to get up early in the morning." She paused, wanting to ask Tai if she had seen the fire, but it seemed a silly question. Fires were not uncommon phenomena on a young world.

"Do you feel it, too?" Tai asked, and searched Lee's face with an intentness unusual for her.

"Feel what?"

"I don't know. Something strong . . . not metal, only a little of it, but it surges. . . ." She paused and then dismissed it all with a shrug. "Wesley Hall says I'm going witchy. Maybe he's right? It happens sometimes. Something in the ground sets me off—like when birds can't navigate." She turned to go. "If you change your mind, come on down. O.K.?"

After she went to bed that night, Lee listened to the breakers crash offshore and wondered if the tide was high. Winds brought snatches of music and party sounds. Perhaps she should have gone, just to be sociable, to keep Tai company. Neither of them were drinkers. She lay there, mulling over Tai's remark about "going witchy." The woman's talent was rare but not unique among people who spent long years in space. She wondered if something in the starships, or in the worlds they visited, altered the biochemistry of thought—something ingested or radiated. Tai's reference to disoriented birds suggested magnetic fields. She fell asleep wondering if Tai could register changes in magnetic fields.

During the night voices and laughter woke her as the party-goers came home. When she got up at dawn, the only sounds in camp were made by birds and insects. She dressed, pocketed her gun and camera, and slipped out for her first real look at this world.

CHAPTER 4

THEY GATHERED ON THE BEACH IN CLUSTERS, LARGE ANIMALS with the great round eyes of deep divers. On Earth she might have called them seals, but here they had no name. They were jade green and shaped like massive swifts, as if they flew the seas.

They watched her with seemingly the same degree of interest that she felt for them, their emerald pupils narrowed to vertical slits against the glare of Xilan's sun, their porpoise-smooth bodies shining in the light.

An hour earlier, when she had reached the cove, it had been empty except for shells and rocks and tidal litter. She had been studying the empty shells when she heard sounds offshore, warbles or yodelings, notes as round as bubbles. At first she could see nothing but breakers rolling green and white, so she sat down to listen.

Individually the sounds were not particularly pretty, but when she stopped concentrating on one and began to hear the whole, things changed. The voices merged with wind and waves and the tumble of the surf. It seemed to her that she could hear songs of a race and world she'd never known, a history murmured by a thousand generations inhabiting this sea, and it was beautiful.

They came then, one by one, planing up out of the waves to lose their grace on the shore. They gathered in groups to study and then to discuss this strange creature who watched them from a respectful distance. In the scope of her camera, she saw their teeth were white and close and sharp, efficient. And while she knew they couldn't digest her without dying, she couldn't assume that they knew that. She wondered what they thought of her, or if they thought at all.

They left as suddenly as they came, turning, crowding one another. The first strokes of their winglike flippers sent water flying in their wake. She frowned; it seemed almost like a rout, as if something had frightened them. Perhaps they hadn't smelled her scent until now? Or they had talked her over and decided she was dangerous? Or maybe some other creature or creatures, enemies, were out there in the water? But in that case—

"Dr. Hamlin?"

The shout startled her. She jumped up to see a field car bouncing over the dunes, recognized the driver as the commander's personal aide, Lieutenant Daniels, and felt a rush of irritation. No wonder the seals were scared—this noisy fool—and then she stopped and thought, They fled before he shouted.

No alien animals were afraid of man until they got to know him, until they'd been shot at for sport or seen their kind reduced to specimens and put into plastic bags. Until they learned otherwise, most were curious and friendly. Man had just arrived on Xilan—how did these creatures know he was a mortal enemy?

"Commander wants you," Daniels called as the car pulled up beside her. "Orientation lecture. He's going to be mad—you're beyond the three-mile limit. How'd you get so far without wheels?"

"I walked," Lee said, preoccupied by musings as she got into the passenger seat. How long had those ships stayed here five hundred years ago?

Daniels waited for her to say more, and when she remained silent, he shrugged. He said no more for the rest of the drive back to camp.

The orientation program was being held in the auditorium of the administration building. A film of the planet was in progress when the two walked in. Like a classroom monitor searching for tardy students, Daniels paused in the doorway and surveyed the crowded little amphitheater. Lee stepped around him and took the nearest empty seat.

"Xilan, a low-gravity, temperate world, is the only life-bearing planet within the Turfan star system," a man's well-modulated voice-over reminded them. "It has three separate continental land masses. Two-thirds of the surface is covered by water. LVL's corporate expedition team established their base camp on the western shore of the smallest and most fertile continent, in the northern hemisphere."

Years from now, Lee guessed, an edited version of this film would be shown as a documentary on the federation circuit. The narrative was totally ubiquitous. LVL was in the heavens; all was right with the world. . . .

The screen went blank, the lights came on, and Commander Nathan rose. He was a plump, gray-haired man, flat-bottomed from years of sitting. His face was furrowed by worry lines and wry with disillusion. Lee had great respect for Nathan. He was a good administrator and kept peace among a crew of people forced to associate with each other for prolonged periods—rather like a too-large family with its inevitable quarrels.

"The first thing I want you all to remember," Nathan began, "is that while we weigh thirty percent less here and this atmosphere is benign, the oxygen mix is thinner than what we're used to. For those born on Earth it's equivalent to an altitude of fourteen thousand feet. So either carry supplemental oxygen until you're acclimated, or take it easy. Two members of our foaming crew are in the medical center with exhaustion. We nearly lost one of them. I don't like it when people make themselves sick through carelessness.

"As with all new worlds, all life forms can be dangerous. Touch nothing without gloves. Preliminary studies show our immuno-logical defense systems ignore Xilan microbes and they ignore us. But we haven't yet learned if there are exceptions. Eat nothing native to this planet. Don't drink unpurified water. Don't pick flowers or pet animals."

He paused to survey his audience and shook his head. "I know some of you will ignore these warnings. Some always do. That is your prerogative. Some are lucky. Some get hurt or die. You are all adults." He waited to let that sink in before going on.

"The *Kekule* will remain in orbit for three weeks to assure our safety here. Once the ship leaves to tour the other planets in this star system, it won't return for six months—surface time. Medical evaluations begin in seven days. If you fail that exam you'll go back to the *Kekule* as standard procedure. If you pass, you can start field work. For the first week everyone is confined to a three-mile radius of this base.

"Regarding work crews . . ."

Lee listened long enough to hear that her group remained unchanged; then she let her mind drift back to the animals in that cove. Had she frightened them? Had the car? On Tanin, animals had flocked around the cars, tried to smell and taste them. Maybe the construction crew had harassed this herd; it was close enough to the base . . .

She woke with a start, head hanging painfully to one side. ". . . your usual close attention," Commander Nathan was saying, in an oddly personal tone. She rubbed her neck and wondered how long she'd been asleep.

"Dr. Hamlin?"

There were two sturdy legs in shiny boots directly to her left. She raised her eyes to take in the rest of the commander.

"Did I disturb you, doctor?"

"No—yes—I'm sorry." She sat up, feeling foolish. The auditorium was empty.

He waved her apology aside. "It's the atmosphere—combined with my orientation lecture. I'd fall asleep myself if I had to listen to it again. But no matter how often you tell some people things, they never listen." He chewed absentmindedly on his lower lip and stared at her hair. "One of the costs in the projected budget on any expedition is: two deaths per every three million of expenditure. When I was younger that was just a statistic to me, but I notice lately that I think about it when I stand up there talking. I look out at all the faces and wonder if some won't be there for our final meeting."

For a moment she thought he was reprimanding her for going beyond the three-mile limit, then decided he wasn't. Nathan never wasted time being subtle.

"That's a morbid thought," she said. "I've been on five expeditions—and we've lost one man. He was killed fighting with a friend."

"We're long overdue."

"Maybe the statistics are wrong. Safety factors improve with each expedition."

He didn't seem to hear her. "The more benign the planet seems, the more careless people get."

Something in his expression reminded her of Tai. Maybe the commander was going witchy too? "What problems did the first ship here encounter five hundred years ago?" she asked.

"None. But they were a private venture," he said. "Private ventures lie a lot on their reports." He turned away and then looked back. "I wouldn't like it if you became a statistic, Dr. Hamlin."

CHAPTER 5

At intervals across the plains are miles of mounds.
Round, grass covered, each is topped by a form that may
be a stylized sculpture of a sentient being. Or may be
something else. They seem to change shape in the dark.
They never look the same. But they are stone.

Her mother's journal, bound in bark and written in mossberry
ink on sheets of handmade paper, lay open on Gareth's lap while
she stared at the fire. She lived alone and, when she was lonely
or upset, found comfort in this book.

The entry had been written twenty years before on a walking
trip her parents had taken into the interior. They had gone north,
up the coast, until cliffs edging the water forced them to turn
inland. They had crossed a narrow range of hills and come out on
a vast flatland.

The journal continued:

We think they're burial mounds. We tried to open one,
without success. They're covered by a thick sod layer, so
uniform it appears deliberate and not the result of wind
drift. Beneath the sod is metal or stone or perhaps an
alloy of the two. Once our people might have known how
to identify this substance. We can't. We tried digging
beneath, but the ground is flint hard. Sometime we'll
come back with the proper tools and learn what's buried
here.

They had never gone back. They used to talk about it sometimes, but they never went. Each time they planned the trip someone got sick and needed care. Neither wanted to go alone or with another person. They had promised they would go when Gareth was old enough to take their place as a medic, but when that time came, both were dying. That was a year ago.

She looked from the green flame sputtering on the logs to the flower that adorned the journal page. Sketched by her mother, the flower seemed to wave jauntily in an invisible wind. The girl bit her lip and closed her eyes. It was little things like this that made her ache with loneliness for them. Sometimes she wished so much to talk with them again, to laugh—

The thought came on impulse, and she didn't dismiss it, because it seemed right—she would go to the mounds, make that the goal of her herb-gathering trip. Now was the ideal time. She would feel no guilt leaving the villagers. Considering the present mood of some of them, it might be wise to go. A month would give them time to recover from their fear. And although she couldn't admit it to herself, they had not only frightened her but deeply hurt her feelings. She wanted nothing to do with them for a while.

She put the journal back into its oilskin case and took it with her as she went to pack. It was after three by the time she'd finished; the hall lights were dim. It was too late to go to bed; besides, she was too excited to sleep. She went out to the slate message board beside the front door and wrote that she had gone on a long herb hunt. After eating a piece of hambread and cheese, she collected her pack, took a lantern, and set off.

Not wanting to raise the gate for fear of waking people, she followed the ramps down to the lowest level of the house and, in the ancient clutter, found the tunnel that led from one of the storerooms, across the compound and out, yards beyond the wall. She hadn't used the tunnel in years and was surprised to find the false boulder sealing the outer door was much lighter than she remembered it. The tunnel was known only to her family—only to her now.

It was that quiet hour between night and dawn when the insects were too chilled to sing, the animals all sleeping. Closing off the lantern's air, she waited for it to dim out, then hid it behind the boulder. Light fog hid the stars. In the darkness she kept bumping into branches. By the time she reached the dunes, her hair and pants legs were dew soaked and her arms were scratched. By sunrise she was five miles north along the beach, beyond all but the most distant fields.

With light the shore became alive with feeding birds and gopahs—small lizards living along the tide line. Purple, green, and blue snails browsed, dragging their turreted shells over the dark sand. Plump crab-like creatures hurried about, alternately being picked up or thrown out by the waves. All was color, noise, and motion.

Warm from her walk, she sat on a boulder to rest and eat some bread and watch the other creatures feed. Flying lizards fished offshore. Like great red diamond kites they glided in wing formation just above the waves. When a fish was spotted, the red wings would fold and they dived arrow-nosed, without a sound. Then they reappeared on the surface and struggled aloft, bottom-heavy with their catch.

Far offshore the fins of something huge passed by, sail-like. She couldn't tell if it was one animal or three, one for each fin, and decided she would probably never know. No one knew much about the open sea and what lived there. The few within memory who'd gone to look had not come back. Once, when she was small, a sixty-five-foot tentacle had washed up on the village beach. It had light sensors on it, or eyes—her parents couldn't be sure. It was very dead.

Although she hadn't slept the night before, she walked all day. Her pack was light, the air cool, and most of all, she wanted to get away, to make the village distant. She camped that night in a cave high above the tide and woke to find her skin prickly with salt crystals. Bathing in the shallows felt good, until she dried and began to itch again.

Frequent reference to the journal told her she was making better time than her parents had. They had reached the bird cliffs in five days; she reached them in four. But then they had had each other for diversion. She had only wild things.

The foothills were a low range, arid and full of salt-tolerant plants. Some plants absorbed so many minerals that their leaves tinkled in a breeze like wind chimes. Other bushes were almost black with tarnish. Here grew carnivorous cacti with hollow spines. The ground around the cacti was littered with mummified remains of insects and small birds trapped and eaten while they were trying to drink the nectar in the plants' thick yellow flowers.

As her parents had done before her, Gareth stopped to gather spines for use as hypodermic needles. Attracted by the noise she made snipping off the needles, blue stonerollers temporarily quit hunting insects and came to watch.

"You're not the prettiest animals," she told them when six had assembled, "or the brightest."

Their heads jerked up at her voice—an alien noise to them. A few made nervous chitterings. They looked like vacuous badgers, with ratty gray fur and pale blue eyes. One ambled toward her and she backed away. It sniffed a string-tied packet and then, satisfied that needles were inedible, sat down again. They didn't bite unless provoked, but Gareth took no chances. A bite would hurt at best and spoil the trip; at worst an infection would send her home.

The cactus grove smelled bad, so as soon as she had finished, she picked up stones and tossed them down the hill behind her to get rid of her audience. No stoneroller worthy of its name could see a rock moving without going to see what insect caused that movement. There was a dusty scramble to investigate. As she left, she looked back to see them fighting over stones they had watched her throw. Stonerollers weren't noted for their cleverness.

She gathered blister weed, boneheal fern, and iron moss, and several pounds of huge clear salt crystals. The crystals she took for their beauty, not because she needed them. Climbing hills took far more energy than walking on a flat beach. When she crossed a streambed where the gravel was blue with turquoise pebbles, she picked up only three prime pieces. Stones grew heavier each day they traveled in backpack or pocket. Someday, she thought, she'd come back here for more.

The journal told of a waterfall from a spring high on a hillside. "The stream is marked with kochia trees, some of them two hundred feet tall, the only green things in these hills," her mother had written. Gareth camped beside the stream that night and washed the salt and dust out of her hair and skin and clothes. While her clothes dried by the fire, she foraged for her supper. She caught what she called trout—three boneless fish that looked like slender snakes. When skewered and slowly roasted, their flesh became delicate and flaky. She dug out the legumes of a reed called pig lily that grew along the stream, and roasted them like potatoes. Dessert was mossberries, past their prime and bitter.

When night came and her fire was the only light, she leaned back against the trunk of a kochia tree for comfort. Her father had told her once that these trees, or trees this tall, were so old that they had been standing here before the first people came. It was possible that her parents had camped beneath them once as she did tonight. And maybe, years from now, her child would walk beneath them. As she thought about it, it didn't seem fair somehow that trees could live so long and people died in forty years or less.

She felt very close to her parents tonight and very grateful to them for giving her life. She would have to have a child soon, she decided, while she was still young and strong. Maybe two, if she could. The problem was choosing a mate. Maxwell would be good. He was intelligent and wise and gentle—and old. Failure would make him feel bad and older still. Oshi was bright, but his mind contained a trace of cruelty. She could not bring herself to imagine such intimacy with him, and she would be suspicious of his child, watching it for its father's trait. Besides, he was a villager. Uri was a possibility; he was a little slow, but he had fathered two bright babies and his parents and grandparents had lived to be quite old. Or Jon . . . perhaps she would try. . . . Considering the pros and cons of various males, she unrolled her fur-lined sleeping bag and went to bed.

The next day she came down out of the hills at sunset and made camp by a tiny spring on a ledge overlooking the plain. Around and directly below her was evergreen forest, the trees stunted and twisted by prevailing northwest winds. Their branches bore fans of long blue-green needles and pink puffs of blossoms topped by a blue crown. Smoke trees, the journal called them.

Beyond the forest stretched a plain and beyond that mountains so high that she could see the sun glinting off the snow peaks. The plain was dotted with grazing herds, vast numbers of animals. Some herds were still drifting as they fed; others had bedded down for the night.

The journal's map was accurate. From the "X" that marked this campsite, arrows indicated mounds to the north and northwest. By squinting into the sun, she could make out their geometric shadow lines.

CHAPTER
6

IT WAS LEE'S DUTY, DURING ORIENTATION WEEK, TO IDENTIFY those local creatures who might prove harmful or pesty and to educate the staff about them.

An element of shock was involved in human exposure to any new planet. The very wildness of the world was threatening. Earth had been paved or cultivated for so long that no living Earthling had ever seen a wild animal, the tangle of a natural forest, or the litter of untended beaches. In fact she thought it probable that if such a crew as this had landed on an unpopulated spot on Earth in the twelfth century, the forest with its bears, panthers, wolves, and wild pigs would have terrified them—to say nothing of wasps and hornets or even the common mosquito-creatures large enough to inflict pain but too small to shoot.

People born in the colonies orbiting Earth and her nearby sister planets had no experience with nature; even their gravity was simulated, and their concept of bad weather was a variance in temperature from comfortable to tepid.

Accordingly, to minimize the shock, care was taken in camp-site selection. The site was rid of native wildlife before construction began. But on prolific planets such as Xilan, no sooner was the camp set up than creatures flew, hopped, walked, or slithered back to their old homes—as if they felt that they belonged there.

Conforming to the basic rule that life evolves in response to the nature of the planet's environment, the creatures of Xilan tended to be large. Hand-size insects were the rule and not the exception as they had been on Earth. Birds the size of eagles were common, as were large flying lizards. Most of the higher animals were furred bipeds, but unlike Earth's kangaroos, their lower legs were not massive and in Xilan's lesser gravity they did not need the counterweight of a thick, muscular tail. Their chests were large to house the large heart and lungs required in this thin atmosphere. They were striders, not hoppers, and they stalked over their green world carrying their bushy tails erect.

The larger animals kept their distance from the camp, Lee noted, and the few she saw seemed to be herbivorous, grazing on the grass and shrubs of the surrounding hills. She knew there had to be predators, but those were apparently more wary of intruders.

Early one morning of that first week, while exploring near the camp, she watched three big striders on a knoll engaged in what appeared to be a simple fight for dominance—or a Xilan version of King of the Hill. Each animal stood ten feet tall and would have weighed half a ton on Earth. They had black pronged horns, black-clawed front feet, and blue fur so thick and shiny that she feared for the species if ever a furrier saw them. They moved like awkward karate fighters, kicking sideways with their hind legs, chopping with the claws, but only once did one try to gore an opponent. Lee thought that move was made in anger because the aggressor immediately stepped back as if it had made a mistake. The other two, turning to chase it, saw her standing there watching. All three went still, their play or enmity forgotten. Long ears went up. One bleated a high-pitched warning, and the trio fled behind the hill. She considered their size and hers and wondered at their fear.

The trees around camp were tall. Most suggested evergreens, with long, delicate needles and clusters of fruit like tiny sulfur-yellow dates. The fruit was ripe. Birds and lizards fed on it, and on the insects attracted by the acidic melon scent. There were tree-size succulents, exotic as boojums, blue, green, or yellow-brown. Some were heavily thorned, others smooth and dimpled, and a few appeared to have warts with long white bristles growing out of them.

If this small section of the world was typical, Lee decided Major Singh was correct—it was a pretty place with little on it to inconvenience humankind and much to recommend it. There were a few obvious drawbacks, but her first impression was that, with common sense combined with caution, Xilan was as benign as it was interesting.

The only immediate nuisances were domed insects that flew like small hot-air balloons. Their wings and the top half of their semisoft shells were nearly transparent and focused sunlight on dark internal organs and bottom shell, which served as heat collectors. At sundown the wings darkened to conserve the heat inside; with dawn, wing color drained away, gases expanded, and the bug floated up to feed on smaller insects, catching them in a trap made of ten sticky, dangling legs. The problem was those legs caused an itchy acid burn on any human skin they touched.

"How can anything so pretty smell so bad?" Major Singh asked when he saw her catch one. The bug sat like a yellow-green bubble on her white gloved hand.

She cautiously bent her head and sniffed. "Off gases and musk!" She studied the creature more closely, then pointed to its clearly visible interior. "Decomposition there sends—"

"Don't explain it to me—O.K.?" he pleaded.

"But it's an elegant system, and you're an engineer."

"It stinks." He rubbed his nose. "And it needs flying lessons. It uses those wings as rudders instead of really flying. Bumps into everything—including us."

"That's why it smells. It can't navigate fast enough to escape predators. I would guess not many creatures could stomach that odor."

"Some can." He pointed to the underbrush. "That fat lizard thing eats them." Before she could protest, he gingerly took her bug and walked over to the bush. "I'll show you. Here, fellow," he called as if summoning a dog. "Here you go, boy—girl, whatever." He waved the bug in the air.

From beneath a broad leaf a plump lizard stepped forward. Mottled blue and green, it blended into the background so well that Lee didn't see the animal until it moved. It was shaped like a tailless wallaby, with a bullet head and round blue eyes that gleamed above a heavy jaw. It peered expectantly at Major Singh and then at the bug; hesitantly one of the small forepaws reached out and clasped the offering.

With the deliberate air of reptiles or of connoisseurs, it opened its hard-gummed mouth, put the bug in whole, and squeezed. The lizard's cheeks puffed out; a loud popping explosion jerked its head sideways and caused its eyes to cross. For a moment it sat stunned and then began to chew, mumbling out fragments of shell and wings. It swallowed, looked up at Major Singh to see if he had more, and then at Lee.

"That thing looks much too alert for a reptile," she decided.

"It couldn't be too smart and still eat those bugs," the major said, and she laughed, but she felt uneasy. Sooner or later she would have to kill and dissect one of those creatures. The more aware the animal seemed, the more difficult that part of her job became. If Xilan's reptiles appeared intelligent, what would the higher animals be like?

"Delicious!" was Wesley Hall's comment when she told him her suspicions later that afternoon. "The computer and I have done extensive analyses on two of the small strider specimens in the lab freezer, and five native grains. The protein in the grain ranges from eleven to twenty-two percent. We *can* eat it. The essential amino acids in the meat compare favorably to those in hen's eggs. The flavor is a little—uh—musky, but then both meat specimens were male."

"If we can eat them, can they eat us?"

"I suspect so . . . if they ever get past our smell."

Because they were professionals, most staff members tolerated, if they did not actually enjoy, the presence of wild creatures. But the only person who appreciated them as much as Lee was Wesley Hall—but for very different reasons. Lee loved them for themselves. Wesley Hall loved them on a platter—preferably with gravy. While she believed that each planet's life evolved to its ultimate unique complexity and ultimately had meaning, Wesley Hall felt life evolved to eat and be eaten. She analyzed and catalogued new species; he tried to turn them into recipes.

If humans were to colonize a world, that world had to be capable of producing food humans could consume and tolerate. Many worlds were spared human colonization because everything that lived on those worlds was toxic to man. Xilan appeared an exception to the rule and thus vulnerable.

"Better yet," Wesley Hall went on, "Nathan's relaxed the rules a bit—after some abject begging on my part. He gave permission for the three of us—you, Tai, and me—to go joyriding tomorrow, provided we take a nonscientific type along to ride shotgun. We have our choice of Singh—who needs a break from stress —or Lieutenant Daniels, who has also passed his medical and is driving Nathan crazy organizing the office."

"I vote for the major," Lee said quickly.

"So did I." Wes grinned. "Daniels makes me feel old and frivolous at the same time. I always have this illogical desire to break his nose."

"How far are we allowed to go?"

Wes shrugged. "We have to be back by five p.m."

"That's not long, but at least we can scout the coastline and get some idea of where we want to set up field camps."

CHAPTER
7

THE SLOPE OF THE MOUND MADE A NATURAL BACKREST. GAReth leaned against it, as relaxed as in her bed. The mounds were all and more than she had expected them to be—and she had expected a lot.

She had walked among them all that afternoon, admiring them, puzzling over what they were or what they represented, and intrigued by the fact that there were no animals here, not even insects. She had counted one hundred and eighty-one mounds in this grouping and suspected they were arranged in the shape of a spiral. One hundred and eighty of them were covered with a fine grass so uniform it appeared clipped. The last mound in the spiral's tail was bare and was the one her parents had tried to excavate and had failed.

When she came upon it, she had stopped still, then squatted down and placed her hands palms down on the stone, as if in touching she could somehow feel and share what had been felt here twenty years ago. But the stone was cool and impersonally dry and retained no memory. She clapped the dust from her hands and stood up, feeling slightly foolish.

The sculptures that adorned each mound were strange roughhewn things. They were not human figures, but they didn't look like any animal Gareth had ever seen or could imagine. Some had furry hands or paws, and some wore garments and hats. Twelve were holding what could have been books. Many were knob-headed things with slits for eyes and wheels for legs, and there were pyramid shapes with petal-pointed eyes and ears.

Imaginary creatures, she decided, but from what sort of imagination?

The geometric symmetry of the mounds pleased her as much as the great cube's design or the salt crystals, and it occurred to her, as she lay there watching the stars come out, that there was something missing in the way her people lived. The Builders had known something about design; they had paid attention to what pleased the eyes and, by so pleasing, had freed the mind to dance. The people now were very different, and she didn't understand why.

Something moved. She saw it from the corner of her eye—a shape changing, shimmering up. But when she looked directly at it, all was still. She got up slowly, noiselessly, and began to walk. The only sound was the grass brushing against her legs. The statues stood as still as stone. She climbed up and touched several to make sure.

She watched them for a time and then returned to the comfort of her sleeping bag. The night air was cold. Perhaps what looked like motion was simply heat waves escaping from the stone, distorting the air. She yawned, and her eyes teared. The figure on the mound across from her became a shape that flowed up and down a central axis. There was a rhythm to it, as regular as a clock. Maybe it was all part of the design, she thought. Maybe that was why the cube moved at night, too? She didn't understand the reasoning behind it, but it seemed to make some kind of sense.

High overhead a star passed much too quickly across the sky. Gareth didn't see it, having fallen asleep.

A tremendous gust of wind and a rushing noise woke her. Her first groggy thought was, Tornado! Dust and tiny stones were flying, and she pulled the fur over her head to escape being cut or blinded. But even as she did so, her mind registered three things: the sun was up, there were no clouds, and in that one brief glimpse she had seen a huge shadow flick across the mounds.

She lay there wondering, frightened, and finally grew brave enough to risk peeking out. The tasselated grass, heavy with dew, leaned to the west. Some had been pushed flat. The rushing noise had moved off but was still loud. She saw the grass begin to quiver, and closed her eyes as the thing passed overhead again, and then, abruptly, all was quiet.

Only the matted grass gave evidence that she had not dreamed the entire thing. She got up slowly and looked around. Nothing. She felt a sense of disappointment; something extraordinary had passed by, and fear had made her miss seeing what it was.

An hour later she had almost forgotten the incident, involved instead with the mystery of the mounds and how to penetrate the one her parents had denuded. Since they had failed with a hatchet and a shovel, she had considered the problem and come to the conclusion that if the stony ground couldn't be dug, perhaps it could be brushed away. Accordingly, she sat cross-legged, using a hand broom to whisk away the soil and patiently pick out the gravel and boulders as they were uncovered. It was slow work, but she already had a hole some two feet wide and ten inches deep along the mound's base, and she was beginning to suspect the structure was shaped like a pot with a high-domed lid.

Pausing to rest and let the dust settle, she pulled some grass and began to braid it into a string to tie her hair back from her face. As she did so, she thought she heard voices.

The grass stopped rustling between her fingers; her breathing quickened and went shallow. A voice called, another answered, and a third joined in. The words were unintelligible, fast and gabbling. Strange as the phenomenon was, after the first shock she wasn't frightened. The voices sounded like those echoing inside the cube.

As she listened, she went on braiding the grasses and wondered if the cube and mounds could somehow be linked. Both were products of people who had been capable of doing extraordinary things. These voices sounded more real than those in the cube, she decided, and wondered if she could find the machines that made the sounds. They might be hidden in the sculptures to make them seem more real—or to frighten away animals? But her parents never mentioned hearing voices here. As she tied the grass braid around her hair, she decided she would investigate.

Five mounds down and two to the left, she turned and headed toward the outer ring of the spiral.

"Look at this one!"

Gareth stopped still. The voice was nearby, the sound startlingly lifelike. And the words almost made sense to her.

"Are they totems?"

"I hope so. I'd hate to think they were done from life."

"What's Dr. Kim doing?"

"Communing with the ground."

"Oh. I never saw anyone do that."

"She says whatever makes her witchy comes from here."

Two voices, man and woman, talking in casual tones that wouldn't frighten anything. Gareth started to climb the nearest mound and look over, then on instinct dropped to her knees and crawled up as silently as possible.

The first thing she saw was a bright yellow machine sitting in the center of a circle of flattened grass and, directly below, walking slowly along the outer row of mounds, two people. Beyond them were two more. She dropped flat onto the grass and tried to understand.

They were strangers, dressed in strange bright clothing. Where had they come from? There were no people in the world except those in the compound and the village. There was an old children's story about people who had flown away to escape a sickness and built a wondrous village somewhere, but it was make-believe, a myth of the Builders. Maybe it was true? That machine had to fly to get here; it had no wheels.

She tried to remember all the old stories, how it was said the first people were small yet very powerful. She raised her head and parted the grass to look at the strangers. Three were no more than five feet tall, one a head taller, their skins a light golden brown. Their clothing was beautiful, close-fitting and of shades she'd never seen except on flowers, and she wondered how they made those dyes.

A stranger with a woman's voice reached down and took something from her belt. Gareth recognized a mask of the type she'd seen in the storerooms beneath her house, among things her parents said were as old as the house. The woman held the mask up to her face.

Gareth ducked down again to consider this; it was possible these *were* descendants of the Builders. She couldn't think of any other explanation. The stories said they'd gone away or died off or disappeared—but all the stories differed. If some people had left the village long ago, they wouldn't have had to go far never to be seen again. Two hundred miles would insure total isolation. If they had, and these were their descendants, they would be glad to learn that the compound and the village still existed. And that she was distantly related to them.

She rose to her knees, intending to go out and introduce herself, then looked down at her clothing and paused. They looked so splendid compared to her, so clean and clipped. Oh, well, it couldn't be helped. If these people were bright enough to fly, they'd be bright enough to know you couldn't go camping and look your best. And maybe they could explain the mounds once they could talk to her.

She pushed herself erect on the steep little hill, walked to the top and, holding the knob-headed statue with one hand to keep from slipping, called out to them.

"You there! Where are you from?"

Three of them stared up at her, open-mouthed. The tallest reached for something worn on his belt. The fourth, a plump woman kneeling on a nearby mound, looking as if she were listening to its insides, glanced up and then went back to listening for a moment more before looking at Gareth again. The girl heard her say very distinctly, "Ohmigawd," as if the word were sacred.

CHAPTER
8

"SHE'S BEAUTIFUL!" SAID MAJOR SINGH.

"She's human!" said Wesley Hall.

Through her camera Lee stared up at this apparition who stood atop the mound like some ancient tribal priestess questioning their right to trespass. The mounds were some twenty feet high, the statues five feet tall. This young woman, if that was what she was, was more than six feet tall. She was dressed in rust brown: an ill-fitting sleeveless tunic, skintight trousers, and knee-high boots. All appeared to be handmade.

But what struck Lee most was the creature's skeletal structure; it had quite the finest bones she'd ever seen—as if a sculptor had stretched the human frame to its ultimate extension, then chiseled an ideal. That long bare brown arm and narrow long-fingered hand resting on the statue possessed an airy grace. Out of training and habit, Lee tried to estimate the bones' tensile strength, the lift capacity of the muscles in this atmosphere. It was difficult to judge because of the tunic, but the rib cage appeared disproportionately large, a flaw in the sculptor's design.

She focused on the face. Pale skin made paler by black hair and eyebrows, gray-blue eyes, wide-set and very clear; a nose that could be termed aquiline but might with age be hawkish; good mouth and chin. The right canine tooth should have been aligned in childhood.

Lowering her camera, she met intelligent eyes and saw not hostility but curiosity mingled with uncertainty and a sort of childlike trust that touched her heart and set her mind to racing.

She later said it was the strain of staring up into the morning sunshine that caused her eyes to fill.

"They colonized!" Her voice was an awed whisper.

"What?" Major Singh frowned at the tears in her eyes but didn't presume to question.

"Five hundred years ago—the private venture—those ships *colonized* this world. That's why the animals run from us. . . ." She was still staring at the girl. "Can you understand me?"

The girl frowned slightly, then shook her head, not really comprehending.

"You think she speaks our language?" Singh was skeptical. The girl glanced at him, then looked to Lee again, eyes questioning.

"I thought I heard her say, 'You there.'" Tai had come to join the trio staring upward. "If they were colonists, then she might speak a form of our language as it was spoken five hundred years ago. As we do. But our different derivations are going to be a problem."

"I'll get the translating unit." Major Singh turned to go back to the airtruck. "And I'd better tell Nathan about this."

Lee reached out and caught his arm. "No—wait."

"She's right," Wesley Hall agreed. "We call the base and we'll start a real ruckus. In fifteen minutes this place will be swarming with people. Let's get acquainted first."

"I'll get the translator." Singh set off at a run.

"Where did she come from? We didn't fly over any towns—"

"Maybe south of here," Wes interrupted Tai. "Suppose they've adapted to an all-native diet? Would that explain her looks? No colony's been able to go completely native. I can hardly wait to see her test results—she'll save us weeks of work! And there must be more like her."

While they talked, Lee watched the girl study them, her eyes moving from speaker to speaker as if she were truly listening. She *cannot* understand us, Lee thought, for if she did she would turn and run. The gray-blue eyes met hers again, and on sympathetic impulse Lee smiled. The girl hesitated, then a look of relief came over her face, and she started slowly down the embankment toward them.

"Watch it!" Wesley Hall began to back away. "She's big enough to hurt us if we frighten her."

The girl paused in midstep, nearly tripped forward, but then regained her balance. She looked from Lee to Wesley Hall, and her smile faded to a wryly puzzled expression.

Damn you, Wes, Lee thought. People always talk too much, always frighten wild things. If there's any hope of gaining trust, some fool always talks. She held out her hand in welcome now, but the girl ignored the gesture and retreated slowly to the top of the mound.

How small they are, Gareth thought, and how disappointing. They're afraid of me, as the villagers are afraid of the cube. Perhaps if I get too close they'll throw rocks.

The legendary people who built the cube had always seemed more than human to her. For some reason she kept thinking of a phrase from one of her favorite stories. ". . . and the gods left the world and took the road to heaven." As a child she'd always pictured them leaving the compound, walking out the gate and down the hard road. In her imagination they had been much more impressive than these people.

In the near distance a herd of white-tailed grazers raised their heads and then stood up, attracted by the voices, curious to see what animal was talking. They milled about uneasily until one lost its nerve and bolted. The rest of the herd followed. Gareth, watching them run, thought it might be wise to follow. There was still time. They'd never catch her; their legs were much too short. But that machine flew. She might be able to reach the trees and hide until they went back to wherever they had come from. But she wouldn't learn anything that way, or ever understand about them or the mounds or their cube—or why her people had been left behind. The risk of losing this potential for knowledge gave her a desperate courage.

She knelt on one knee to make her height less intimidating, as one did with children or with pets. "I am Gareth Mitchell," she told the woman with the sad eyes. She spoke very slowly. "My name is Gareth Mitchell."

"Does she lisp?"

"Sh!"

Gareth ignored the couple and kept her gaze fixed on the woman's face. Perhaps too many sounds were confusing? Feeling rather absurd as she did so, she pointed to herself and edited her message, "Gareth Mitchell," and waited while the woman slowly repeated the syllables, then said them in a rush.

"Gareth Mitchell!" She pointed excitedly at Gareth. "Your name?"

Gareth nodded and was rewarded with a smile.

"Lee Hamlin." The woman pointed to herself and repeated the name.

It took tedious minutes to learn just their names, and Gareth began to wonder how long it would take to learn anything that mattered. The tall one returned, carrying a small blue box. She learned his name.

Her knees ached from crouching on the incline, and when one leg started to cramp, she stood up. They backed away, and she nearly laughed. That people who could fly should fear her was more silly than insulting. She sat down and patted the grass beside her as an invitation for them to join her.

Lee hesitated, then sat six feet away. The other three exchanged glances. The tall one came up and sat beside Lee.

Gareth looked him over and wondered how long his parents had lived and if he had ever sired a child. She pointed to the shiny fabric of his sleeve. "Name?"

"Shirt," he said. "Shirt." He pointed to Gareth's tunic to reinforce the idea. "Shirt."

Then "boots" and "hands" and on through an inventory of everything around them, grass and mounds, sky and clouds, until it became clear to Gareth that these strangers still used many of the same words. They just said them differently.

"Where do you live?" she asked, and they pointed north.

"How far?"

"Ten minutes," said Singh.

"Two hundred miles," said Lee.

Gareth thought that over. It made no sense to her. She decided to ignore it. "Why did you leave the compound?" They didn't understand the question, no matter how slowly she repeated it, and their answer again confused her. She thought they were saying, "The weak was up," which made no sense at all.

"Why did you go away from *our* compound?"

Lee frowned, and looked to the other three for help.

Wesley Hall pointed upward. "We come from sky," he said, and Lee Hamlin laughed. It was such a nice laugh that it distracted Gareth's thoughts. The man was apparently making a joke.

A yellow button lighted on the blue box and a new voice said, "Translation capacity now seventy percent."

"That's enough to make ourselves understood," said Tai.

"Or misunderstood," said Lee.

The box dutifully translated their words for Gareth and thus revealed its function to her. She thought it resembled some of the junk in the storerooms, the things Paul took apart for the metals and fine wire thread they contained.

"This makes what I say clear—understood—by you?"

"Yes."

"And I can understand you?"

"We hope so."

She immediately began to repeat her questions: Why had their people left the compound in the distant past? Why had they never returned? Why were they here now? The answers she got were as confusing as they had been before.

"This thing doesn't work very well," she decided, pointing to the translator. "It's telling me you're saying you come from a compound of your own and before that you came from a distant star. I don't want to hear your legends. . . ." She decided that wasn't tactful. "Later I would like to hear them, of course, but now I'd like to know . . ." and she repeated her questions again.

"Perhaps it would be easier if you told us where your people came from and how long they have lived here," Lee suggested. "You are as big a surprise to us as we are to you."

"Truly?"

"Yes."

Gareth considered that. Had they forgotten their past, too? Looking at the airtruck and the translator, she found it difficult to believe these people had forgotten so much.

"We don't know much of our past, not much we're sure is true." She wrapped her arms around her knees as a brace against the slope. "Our legends say that long ago there were people called the Builders who could do almost anything—as if they possessed magic, but they did it with machines. They went away. We don't know why. Many years passed and people forgot; people died. Knowledge died with them. Some of us believe people used to live much longer than we do now and had more time to learn and teach."

"How long do your people live?" asked Wesley Hall.

"A long time—a few get to be fifty."

Again looks were exchanged, the significance of which escaped Gareth until she thought to ask, "How long do your people live?"

"At least twice—"

Lee interrupted, "Somewhat longer. Are your parents still living?"

"No. They were medics," Gareth explained. "They died at forty, but they had to work too hard. I'm the medic now, the only one . . ." She paused, reminded again of the need to train someone to help her. Whispering made her glance up to see them looking at her with great sympathy—as if they'd known her parents. She had not expected this sort of understanding and wondered if she had underestimated them. Still, their reaction seemed excessive for someone they had never met, unless . . . an embarrassing thought struck her.

"This place, is it your burial grounds? Is that why you came here today—to visit graves?"

"Is *that* what this place is?" asked Tai. She sounded dubious.

Gareth frowned. "I don't know. I thought you did. I thought your people built it, the way they built the cube."

"What cube?"

It took more than an hour for her to explain. By the time she'd answered their questions, she'd told them much about the life of the compound and the village, plus a great deal about herself. And she still had learned very little.

"You're being unfair," she protested. "You ask questions faster than I can answer, and you've told me nothing about yourselves."

"She's right," said Lee. "We're not being fair."

"I told her where we came from and she didn't believe me," protested Wesley Hall.

"No wonder—'We come from sky,'" Tai mimicked in disgust, "as if she were some ignorant savage." She turned to Gareth. "We are part of a corporate research team sent out from the Perth main base in L₅ to study Xilan. Our ship reached orbit ten days ago. We'll be here for six months, learning everything we can about this planet. You're going to be a lot of help, you and your people. Just knowing colonists have survived all this time is—"

Gareth turned to Lee. "What is she talking about?" and then listened silently to Lee's explanation.

"That's impossible," she said when she understood.

CHAPTER 9

THE PROBLEM WAS GARETH DID BELIEVE IT, OR AT LEAST THAT part she understood. It explained things that had made no sense before. Still, "If we came from another world, if something so strange was true, surely we would know it, retain some legend of it?"

"Not necessarily," Lee said. "The colony might have been hit with disease, storms, starvation. Any number of things could have killed most of the original settlers. Failed colonies are an old story in Earth's history. Advanced cultures died in a decade or less; the survivors retained little or none of the knowledge held by the generation before. If your computers went down—"

The woman was talking too fast for Gareth to grasp what she heard. A peripheral area of her mind registered the strangers' scent and wondered if she smelled as odd to them. They didn't smell bad, not of fear or fever, but foreign, as if they'd never eaten the foods she ate, never bathed with tallow soap. How thick their bones were, and their noses—She forced herself to try to concentrate on what they were saying.

"We can prove it." Wesley Hall pointed toward the yellow machine. "We can take you with us."

"No!" Lee turned off the translator. "Aside from the fact that she might not want to come, if we take her back with us the moment she steps out of the airtruck and they see her towering over us, she becomes a Xilan specimen. Exhibit A, to be harassed in the name of science. Try to put yourself in her place."

"I agree," said Singh. "It's not fair to hand her over to those egocentrics."

"Be realistic," Wes said. "It can't be avoided. The moment she said hello she became a specimen, as did all her people. It's just a matter of time."

"Suppose we go see her colony," suggested Tai, "and let them see us. That way the shock won't be so great when the others come."

"You mean now?" Singh asked, and when Tai nodded, "That might be dangerous. They sound a little backward, and they might not appreciate our just dropping in. I'd hate to risk it without letting the base know where we're going and why. I'm your security detail," he reminded them.

"We're armed—besides, the girl is friendly," Wesley Hall argued.

Gareth waited for the translator to repeat their conversations. When it didn't, she became uneasy. They were talking now as if she weren't here. Whoever or whatever they were, she suspected she was not quite real to them, not quite human. The rudeness of them, the disregard, angered her. She stood up—and they got up so fast they stumbled down the slope. One never trusted an unknown animal.

The translator was turned on again. "We'd like to see your home—the village where you live," Lee said. "And the building you call the cube."

"When?" Gareth asked, but she already knew the answer.

"Now—today. We'll go anyhow but if you'll go with us, we'll very much appreciate it. We'd bring you back here before sunset."

"What would you do there?"

"Just observe, and talk to your people—if they'll let us. We won't harm anything."

The airtruck was warm from the sun. When Singh opened the

hatch, the air inside breathed out scents of fabric, metals, and plastics mingled with faint cosmetic odors and a hint of the lunch the four had brought along. Gareth's nose tingled, and she sneezed.

Bending low, she stepped in and wedged herself into a seat. Her knees thrust up at an uncomfortable angle; the headrest ended at the base of her neck, and her hair brushed the roof.

The hiss of jets frightened her, and she felt her pulse throb in her knees jammed against the seat ahead. The ground began to move past the windows and then fell away as the craft lifted. The sensation was disorienting. Looking down, she nearly cried out to see how high she was. The craft turned; the mounds came into view, and her pleasure at seeing a theory confirmed outweighed her fear. "It *is* a spiral! A spiral with a fantail!"

"What did you say?" Lee asked. Gareth glanced over at her and decided it was too involved to explain. She shook her head and turned back to the window.

To her disappointment, the mounds had disappeared, replaced by green and brown shadowed undulations. The foothills that had taken her two days to walk across were made insignificant by this height and speed. She turned and looked the other way and saw the plains, the herds reduced to tiny dots of color. Up here the view was all; there was no feel of the ground, no smells of soil or vegetation, no animals to watch, no insect or flower to be admired. As she thought about it, for the first time it occurred to her how different these people's perspective, their view of the world and of things in general, must be.

It had taken her six days to walk the hundred-odd miles to the mounds. The flight back took ten minutes. She saw the cube come into view and the geometric pattern of the fields stretching across the valley to the compound. It all looked tiny, different —and vulnerable.

"Look there!" Major Singh pointed. "Look at the size of that thing!"

"It's an MMT . . . isn't it?"

"I never saw one that big!"

Gareth's shoulder touched the window as the airtruck banked. The sea flashed into view with village women fishing in the surf.

She saw a woman look up at them and point; the face contorted in a yell, and other faces turned upward. They looked more shocked than frightened. She was going to say so to Lee, but the four of them were staring out the other side, preoccupied with the cube.

"Why did they put a telescope that size on Xilan? Who or what were they monitoring?"

"They've learned to streamline them since that was built."

"Yet from what Gareth said, it could still track the *Kekule*—or our shuttles—"

"It would have automatic realignment, self-control."

"Yes, but she said voices came from inside."

"Could be bearings screeching. That thing's old."

"Let's circle out over the water, get the hills behind it, so the cameras get it in perspective," Wesley Hall suggested, and Gareth's view changed to the sea.

"We're scaring the birds or whatever is nesting on the cliffs." The major swerved to avoid collision with a flock of seabirds and narrowly missed a head-on impact with a kite glider. For an instant a cold yellow reptilian eye glared at Gareth from just outside her window, and then her view was obscured by a leathery red wing. There was a muffled *clunk* against the underside of the craft. She pressed her cheek against the pane and saw the glider falling in a barrel roll, one wing broken and useless. It hit the sea and disappeared without a splash.

"There's the village—over there! And people!" Lee called out, and the other three looked down. For minutes no one said a word.

The houses looked so small from up here, Gareth thought, but neat and ordered, each with its stone fence. And she could see all of the road, from the beach, through the village and fields and across the valley to the mill.

"But . . . what kind of colony is *that*?" Wesley Hall broke the silence. "Where is everything? Where's the sewage recycle plant? Or the power plant? The greenhouses? Do you see any outdoor lighting? There's a traction *animal* pulling a two-wheeled —thing—and a windmill?" His voice trailed off in disbelief. The translator conveyed only his words, but Gareth heard his tone.

"It's what Gareth said it was," Lee reminded them. "We simply didn't imagine what it would look like in reality. For some reason, they regressed."

"That far?"

The expressions on the faces of these four looked as shocked and unbelieving as the village women on the beach, and Gareth found that odd. For if what they said was true—that her people had come from their world, that her ancestors were also theirs and had built the cube—then seeing this should not surprise them. And yet it did.

At her direction, they flew across the valley and landed in the compound just inside the gate, where no trees grew. They let her get out first, either from courtesy or fear—she wasn't sure which. Her knees almost buckled as she stepped to the ground. She was trembling both from delayed reaction to the flight and nervous anticipation of the reception these visitors might get. The first thing she did was to close the gate. She wanted no visitors from the village; it would be hard enough explaining things to Paul and the others here.

CHAPTER 10

"WAIT HERE," THE GIRL HAD SAID BEFORE SHE DISAPPEARED beneath an ivy-covered archway. The four of them obeyed. They stood beside the airtruck, ill at ease. The walls of ruined buildings gaped down at them and shut out the wind. The midmorning sun was hot. In the stillness the airtruck clicked to itself.

"Eerie, isn't it?" Tai whispered. "It's like seeing our base years from now. All the people gone. Buildings rotting into ruin."

"Maybe this wasn't a colony but a marooned expedition." Wesley Hall was whispering, too, Lee noted. But then the occasion seemed to call for whispers.

"Too many permanent structures." Major Singh's face was half hidden by his camera. "There was room to house a thousand people here, maybe more."

Why am I not filming this? Lee wondered. It's the proper thing to do, detached, impersonal. Recording first impressions of a find of great scientific and historic value—the discovery of a lost colony? Why do I feel we're intruders? And that we're being watched? Seeking the reassurance of the familiar, she leaned against the airtruck.

Trees had grown up to shield what remained of the administration building. An antique Comsat dish still stood atop the tower but was oddly tilted, as if support struts had given away. Something had built a large, untidy nest of twigs in the bowl. On the building's sagging roof fragments of the solar collector glinted like bits of a ruined mosaic. An antiquated dome stood where the research lab was usually located. Thickets grew inside crumbling walls that might have once housed scientists. Worn paths meandered across the green. But she saw no people.

A softly constant splashing crept into her awareness. Ignoring Singh's frown, she crossed the open area and walked a short way down the main path. There was a fountain, or what remained of one. Reeds choked one end. The pool was thick with waterweeds, but in the center a vitreous pipe still burbled. Shadows glided beneath the water's surface. She sat on the mossy stone rim, reached down into the water, and felt a glass pool liner slippery with algae. Something dark swam toward her, and she quickly jerked her hand out.

There was a distinct odor to the place, a mixture of deep shade, humus, decaying stone, and mud—the normal smells of a woodland pond, not unpleasant, but very alien to her.

Somewhere close by, a chicken clucked a warning. What appeared to be five big red hens were peering at her, beady-eyed, from a dust bed under nearby bushes. When she stared at them, they stood up, nervously fluffed the dust from their feathers, and prepared to scatter if she made a move.

It was not she who made them run, but a tall, white-haired man in brown who came strolling down the path. He didn't see her because he was looking at the truck. Her first impression was that she had never seen a more gentle face. He looked like someone blessed with peace. There was a glow about him, an almost translucent quality to his skin. Gareth was slender; this man was thin to the point of fragility—so thin that she felt a rush of worry for him, wondering what ailed him.

She tried to think what she would feel if she were in his place, if suddenly an aircraft landed in a world that had no aircraft, and she decided she would probably hide and watch until she saw what they wanted. This man, like Gareth, was coming out to meet them. Were they so brave, these people, or so innocent, like animals that have never known predators?

He accidentally kicked a pebble toward the hens, and they

exploded into flight with squawks of panic. He sidestepped to avoid one, and another crashed against his leg and squawked again. One hit a tree and fell into a lurching run, while two took refuge beneath a bush. "No one is going to hurt you," he assured them, and then he saw her and stopped still in shock. The smile provoked by the chickens faded.

"I locked the truck," she heard Singh say, and turned to see the others approaching, Gareth looking like a young mother with three old children in tow.

"Gareth!" There were both surprise and relief in the man's voice.

The girl ran to greet him with a hug, and the two stood talking, holding hands. She could be his child, Lee thought; the physical resemblance was so strong. But with a limited breeding population they might all look alike. Gareth did most of the talking; he listened and calmly regarded the visitors and the airtruck, as if—now that the initial shock was over—he were at ease with the idea of them. At intervals he would nod or ask a question. Then, apparently feeling she had been rude, Gareth turned and beckoned them to join her.

"This is Paul," she said after she had named them for his benefit. "He's our finest craftsman and the keeper of craft books. He can make an ax that never causes blisters, or build a clock from wood and stone."

None of the four had ever used an ax or seen time told by more than glowing digits. They couldn't appreciate the man's accomplishments. Lee saw he seemed to realize this because he smiled at their incomprehension. Like a good host he turned the conversation to a topic his guests could understand.

"You believe we came here from a distant star—as you have? That your people and ours were once alike? That your people were once, long ago, the race we call the Builders?" he asked Lee.

"Yes. All of that."

"Why do you believe that?"

"Because you're human. Only Earth's evolution produced humans. Your language is ours. Your buildings are familiar to us."

"Earth is what you call your world?"

"Yes. And Gareth says you call this planet Xilan—which was Earth's name for it when it was first discovered."

Paul thought this over in the same deliberate manner in which Gareth absorbed information. "You would replace the mystery of our past with many smaller mysteries," he said.

"I believe we can explain it all in time if your people help us," Lee said.

"A chicken!" Wesley Hall's whisper would have crossed a concert hall. "A tall but earthly chicken! And there are two more! They've altered, too!" He looked torn between wanting to catch a hen and wanting to ask questions about them. Courtesy won out. "Do you have many of those?"

"Maybe a hundred," Gareth said, puzzled by his excitement.

"There are more in the village," Paul added.

"They're healthy? They breed?"

"Oh, yes," said Paul.

"Could I buy one—or barter for it?"

"If you're hungry I'll feed you."

"Oh, no—not to eat—as a specimen. I want to see how chickens adapted to life on Xilan."

Lee watched Paul's face as he listened to the translation—still, absorbed in thought, showing no trace of unease—and she wondered if their arrival here was truly a surprise to him or if he had guessed as much from working with the old equipment. His next question revealed his grasp of the situation.

"Then you must regard us also as specimens?"

"Not as specimens," Wes said too quickly. "As colonists. Our various research teams will want to talk with you. We'll do complete physical exams—that sort of thing. Comparative molecular analyses of your proteins will show any divergence . . . explain why Xilan has changed you physically."

"How do we explain how we look to them?" Tai whispered. "They must think we're midgets."

"Have you come here to stay?" Paul asked Lee.

"No, only to learn if the planet is truly suitable for colonization. Then we will go on. But others may come after us, sometime in the distant future."

"To stay?"

"Yes."

"With all your machines?"

"They would be properly equipped, yes."

Paul turned to Gareth. "Show them the storerooms beneath the compound. Show them the old things. They may know what they are and why they were left to ruin."

There were voices down by the airtruck. Perhaps a dozen people had gathered there, looking, talking, touching the metal as if it might burn. Four of them were of normal height or less—and then Lee realized the short ones must be children.

"I'll go explain who you are." Paul let go of Gareth's hand. "Excuse me." And with a formal little bow, he left them.

"He moves well for a man his age," the major commented as he watched Paul's long, firm strides. "You'd think he was twenty-five."

"He's twenty-nine," Gareth said, and Lee gave an involuntary cry of surprise. "His father died at forty-two, his grandfather at forty-five. I'm told both looked younger than Paul does now." For an unguarded moment her face was sad, and then she said, "I'll show you my home." She led the way to the old administration building.

A weathered wooden door had long ago replaced the original entrance. Gareth tugged it open over a fan-shaped groove worn in the flagstone and politely let her guests enter first.

As she stepped into the cool dimness, a sharp pain shot across Lee's back. She ignored it, knowing its cause to be psychosomatic; she was somehow afraid of this building—it was too old, too long occupied, had absorbed too much human energy.

Like their modern buildings this one had been built of foamed sand. Two lighting panels in the main corridor were still intact, dimly functional. But all the rest of the original equipment was gone, the interior totally remodeled into a rude dwelling.

What Gareth called the clinic was a quaint room with a cushioned table, the walls lined with bottles of leaves and seeds and liquids. There was an ancient microscope, manually operated, with no camera—like a child's first toy—and a traumatic array of cutting instruments, all hand-tooled. To think of their use made Lee queasy; this was what the ancients used before light and sonic instruments.

In the living quarters, in answer to their questions, the girl pointed out pictures her parents had painted, blankets woven from the wool of native animals, carpets made by someone named Margo, a chair a grandparent had carved. Every item had a history, a memory, represented part of what she was, what her people had been.

To Lee, who had spent most of her life in space in structures or starships built and owned by corporations, dressed always in impersonal uniforms, associating with impersonal colleagues, Gareth's world of permanence, of continuity, seemed foreign and too intimate, too confining. Even stranger was the concept of a world where the chief source of energy was human labor, and the data storage and retrieval system consisted of books, handwritten on handmade paper and bound in leather.

The room in which food was prepared contained a wooden handpump for water, and a massive brick fireplace with two ovens and a grill. Gareth had to explain what all this was and how it was used. Wesley Hall got very excited at the idea of cooking with fire inside a building. "Just smell that!" he said as he inhaled. "Years of woodsmoke and real food!"

"Your food is unreal?" Gareth was confused. "What do you eat?"

"Synthetics," Wesley told her. "Chemicals bullied into imitations of the real thing. If you don't know what it is before you eat it, for Heaven's sake don't ask afterwards." All of which left the girl more puzzled than before.

"Your machines do everything for you? Even make your food?" she asked, and when she understood that was true, she said, "How very sad," and all laughed but Wesley.

Unlike modern buildings, this one had two floors and a tower. A freight ramp led down into a subsurface level cut from living rock. Stalactites sparkled from the stone ceiling. Here and there a lighting panel still glowed in the walls, and shadowy hallways opened off the corridors. The place smelled damp and musty, and small breezes blew from nowhere.

Lee always thought of storerooms as brightly lit and automated racks of systems-controlled inventory, packaged, coded, and sterile. These were black rooms, jumbled junk piles scavenged through by generations, things so rotted or oxidized by age that most were beyond identification. Over all were dust, the carapaces of dead beetles, the droppings of small animals, and various tiny bones.

"It's metal," Tai kept saying, her hands hovering over collapsing bins and barrels. "That's high cadmium foam—almost all gone—and that's manganese. They were unhappy, whoever handled that. That's wire."

"Oxygen cylinders." Singh's torch revealed tanks stacked like cordwood, blistered with corrosion and rust.

The four viewed these remains of their world's past technology and became more and more silent.

"I don't know why I expected to find more," Singh said after perhaps a dozen rooms of clutter, "but I did. I know, for example, that our airtruck will be junk in thirty years, fit only to scavenge for parts. But I didn't really appreciate what five hundred years meant until now."

Once, five hundred years ago, Lee thought, a research expedition like ours studied this planet and decided it would be a good place for humans—and then moved on to study other worlds, never thinking what the reality of their decision would become.

"Could we go up? Get out of here? Outside . . ." She suddenly could no longer bear being in this labyrinth, enclosed by stone, by age, by what she saw as tragedy. She wanted sunlight and trees and living things. Nonhuman things.

CHAPTER 11

WHEN SHE CAME OUTSIDE WITH HER VISITORS, IT SOUNDED TO Gareth as if every walla in the compound were excited. Their alarm call, a series of chesty, ascending *houk-houk-houks*, suggested a much larger creature choking to death.

"What animal is *that*?" Lee asked.

Gareth told her. "I think they're barking at your flier. They must have gotten brave enough to sniff it."

"Are they dangerous?"

"They're pets." She gave a piercing whistle, and five wallas came jogging at an eager yet dignified pace across the green.

"It's the lizard you fed the bug to!" Lee said to Major Singh. "See, the same bullet head—" She turned to Gareth. "Why are they called wallas?"

"I don't know—that's what they're called."

"There was a furred animal on Earth that looked somewhat like that. It was called a wallaby. This term could be a corruption of that."

"Oh," said Gareth, more interested in her note still on the chalkboard by the door. She felt a pang of unease, remembering what had prompted her to go off to gather herbs. If some of the villagers suspected her of strange power because she didn't want them to burn the cube, what would they think once they heard she had returned with the people who built it—that she had brought the Builders back to protect what was theirs? The villagers were capable of believing that—in which case they'd either be in awe of her or scared to death.

"Could we see your other animals?" Lee asked, and Gareth led them off in the direction of the little barn where the few animals in the compound were kept.

Where the house seemed to make them ill at ease, outdoors again they were like four inquisitive children. There was nothing that didn't interest them. They peered into all the buildings, poked among the ruins, picked up old corroded things from the ground and, after asking permission, pocketed them. They asked the names of flowers and of trees and people. Major Singh kept looking at things through what he called a camera. He said it recorded what it saw and heard. He often aimed it at Gareth and, as her neighbors joined her tour, at them. Each new arrival brought more questions, and the group's progress toward the barn was slow.

"Some of the village children are pounding on the gate," Margo whispered to her as she joined the group. "They want to know if we're all right. Are we?"

"As long as we keep the gate closed," said Gareth. "I'm afraid of what they'll do when they see what I brought home." She told the older woman of Luther's rage and Ula's resentment.

"How dare they!" Margo was indignant. "After all you've done for them! No one mentioned it to us—do you suppose the other villagers know?"

"They were frightened—"

"That's no excuse. So was I. So was everyone but you. Luther's a fool. His whole family never was too bright—you can trace them down the years." Margo kept the genealogy charts. "I'll tell our people; so far as we're concerned, you're still out in the wild. You never saw these little people and their machine."

She gave Gareth's arm a squeeze and went off to inform her neighbors. Like Gareth, Margo was the last member of a very old family. She and Paul had failed in their attempts to have children, and both refused to mate with others. Which was a shame, Gareth thought as she watched her friend go, a waste of two good minds, to become so attached, so sensitized, that to avoid an hour or a few night's embarrassment they would die barren. She wouldn't allow that to happen to her.

"More chickens!" sang out Wesley Hall as if greeting a group of old friends. Gareth had always taken chickens for granted, but as these strangers talked about the birds and asked questions, she began to understand that chickens were something special. Their heads were tinier; they had no teeth; their bodies were fatter, their feathers softer. They were like no other animal on Xilan, unique, like people.

If the chickens delighted the visitors, the pigs pleased them still more. "We should have guessed," Tai said. "If we could live here, so could real pigs!" The laughter this remark provoked when translated, and Tai's obvious embarrassment, somehow established a common ground, and all relaxed a little.

They said the pigs had come from their world, too, as had the chickens. Lee Hamlin knelt and with a sharp stick sketched on the clay a picture of an earthly pig. It was shorter and heavy-boned, but quite decidedly a pig with personality. The group crowded to see.

"Your mother could draw like that," Paul said, and Gareth nodded. It was a talent she had always wished to have and lacked.

Lee then drew a plump bird she said was one of their chickens and told how on their world chickens were raised by the thousands in separate little cages to keep them from losing weight by exercise. They were fed and kept clean by machines and, when they were big enough, killed and dressed by other machines. "They never see a human," were the words Gareth remembered, and the picture those words evoked struck deep into her mind. She could not imagine people so detached from reality. It frightened her. She was thinking about that and about what Wesley Hall had said about "real food," while Lee drew an animal with a massive head, big ears, four short legs, and a boxy oblong body.

"Do you know what this is?"

"It walks on all four legs?" Uri asked shyly after the others had shaken their heads no. "Like pigs?"

"Yes."

"It could be a sheep—but those all died out long ago," Margo said. "Extinct."

"You once had domestic animals like this?"

"Yes," Uri said. "There's a painting of one in the village, in the Glaser house. Black-and-white animal. And there's an old skull from one over there. Big thing." He borrowed Lee's stick and sketched the skull.

"Cows," said Wesley Hall.

"Why did they die out?" Lee asked.

No one knew.

She drew a walla and then a wallaby, which to Gareth was far too pretty a creature to be related to her insect-catching pet. But the other people now were fascinated, too. Uri sat down and with a stick of his own began to draw animals for the visitors. He was almost as apt as Lee Hamlin.

"You've observed them closely," Lee commented, and he smiled. Gareth had never seen Uri be so pleasant, and she wondered at his behavior. Paul joined in, and Pearl, drawing animals and exchanging names for them. Lee drew a seal like the jade green animals she had seen, and seemed pleased to hear them call it a seal. Gareth, suddenly tired from all the excitement, walked a few yards away and sat down on a crumbling wall.

In the quiet she could hear people calling from outside the gate. She felt a little guilty, knowing they were genuinely worried as well as curious. But they would meet these strangers soon enough—perhaps as soon as the strangers heard there were still more animals in the village. She frowned, not fully understanding this childish preoccupation with animals.

Childish . . . she glanced over at the visitors again, studying their faces. That's what was different about them. Their faces were rounded, the eyes large, the features flatter, like children's faces. And yet she was sure they were all over thirty. It was very odd. Perhaps that explained why they lived longer?

Major Singh caught her eye, smiled, and came over to join her. "May I sit too?" He spoke very slowly.

"Yes."

"Tired?"

"Yes."

"It's the excitement. I'm tired too." He waved a short, thick hand. "I never expected to see all this when we took off this morning."

"What did you take off?"

"Excuse—oh, when we—uh—left our base to go sightseeing."

Without the translator she couldn't grasp that sentence, and their conversation lagged. A few very long minutes passed, during which she stared at his hands and considered how many of her fingers would equal one of his in weight. Three, she decided. A walla came over to sniff at his boots, and he waved it away.

"Do you believe us?" he asked finally.

"About where our people came from?"

"Yes."

"I suppose so," she said. "I can't really understand the idea of your coming so far—of our ancestors doing that. I can't understand why people would do it."

He tried to explain why, how his people had learned to do extraordinary things, how his world's deserts expanded, how life in the oceans died, how it became necessary for them to build artificial worlds that orbited the mother planet, advancing farther and farther into space until they had to search for new worlds to colonize, like Xilan.

Gareth shook her head. "You *had* to do all that?" she asked.

"Yes. There are just too many people. They had to go someplace. We have to find room for them—"

"You're very fertile?"

He grinned at the word. "I guess you could call us that."

"That's very good," she said. "We're not. How many children have you sired?"

He stared up at her as if the question confused him. "You mean me, personally?"

"Yes."

"None, that I know of. I try to . . ." He paused, embarrassed, and she regretted asking him the question. Some people were so ashamed of being sterile.

"I'm sorry," she apologized. "You can't help it. It's not your fault."

"You don't understand," he said. "We practice birth control. Most of us never have a child—not those who travel space."

It was her turn to stare, not understanding. "Then what's the point of all your lives? Whom do you teach? Who inherits your knowledge—or your land, your beloved things? To be alone . . . Why would you look for other worlds if your own child is never born to live there?"

He paused to think and then shrugged with forced careless-ness. "Someone has to do it," he said. "You can't stop progress . . ."

"That is progress?"

He glanced up at her as if to see if she was being sarcastic, and then looked away, at the barnyard around them, at the pigs and chickens and the people. For a moment his confidence seemed to leave him, and he looked afraid. She couldn't imagine what frightened him, and she searched the ground and wall for bugs or lizards.

"That's what they call it," he said. "It doesn't always work. I'm sorry. I shouldn't get involved," and he abruptly got up and went to join the others.

They left her there beside the mounds where she'd first seen them. It was late afternoon. She stood and watched the departing airtruck become a soundless dot against the sky, and then walked back to her special mound and sat and stared into the shallow hole she'd dug and wondered what she'd brought upon herself and everyone she knew.

CHAPTER 12

FOR THE NEXT TWO DAYS GARETH DUG AROUND THAT MOUND as systematically as a machine: two feet wide, two feet deep, search the base wall for a door seam, sweep a new hole, fill in the old. The days were clear, the nights crisp and cool. She was barely aware of externals. She ate when hunger forced her to, slept when it grew too dark to see. Her hair and skin and clothing became chalky with dust. She was in shock, although she could not realize that until recovery began and she could allow herself to think.

On the third day she fell asleep digging and was wakened by the sun in her eyes the following morning. She found herself curled up beside the pile of sand and stones she'd excavated, her cheek pillowed on the now stubby whisk, her fingertips and knuckles scuffed and cut. Dew settling on her skin had turned the layer of dust into a film of itchy mud.

Staring down at the portion of herself that she could view, she was alarmed at such physical disarray. She was a medic, and medics did not get filthy dirty. She staggered the quarter mile or so through the grass to the tree line where a creek flowed, managed to remove her boots, and waded in to bathe, fully dressed.

Fish fled. A yellow strider drinking on the opposite bank stared in alarm and flicked its tail, squirrel-like, not sure if it should run. A purple gopah trilled a warning to its thirty amphibious children, who then headed for the shallows. In the reeds downstream a widemouthed rufous peered out of its nest, nervous for its own late brood. The interloper showed no tendency to feed but splashed noisily in bathing. It so stirred up the bottom that the strider, who had no taste for sediment, moved upstream in disgust.

Chilled by the night spent outside her sleeping bag, Gareth shivered so that she could hardly bathe. Teeth chattering, she washed off the grime and soaked her long black hair until it fell in squeaky ribbons. The water stung the abrasions on her hands that had begun to heal. But by the time she waded back to the bank to reclaim her dusty boots, she was again a thinking creature.

After spreading her clothes on the mound to dry, she took her comb from her pack and, sitting on her sleeping bag, combed the snarls out of her hair until it dried in waves on her bare shoulders. As she combed, she let her mind accept what was.

She had come to find these mounds as a gesture to the past, a touchstone to her parents, to the surety of childhood, the knowledge that when danger threatened she could curl up in comforting arms and be held safe. But by coming here she had found a very different past. She had gone out to meet it, and now not only was it too late to run, but there was no one left to run to. This was how it would be; for the rest of her life, she would be her own security—or lack of it.

Six months, they said, then they would go. And because it was so far to their world, there was a chance that none of their kind would come again in her lifetime. Gareth didn't know why that thought pleased her, but it did. Smiling, she got up and dressed and surveyed her work.

The mound looked as if it had been circled by an insane mole. The bedraggled sod she'd dug up was dying from lack of rain. There was the shallow pit where the digging stopped. For all that work, she'd discovered nothing new. Perhaps it was just as well; the mounds should remain her parents' mystery. If the woman,

Tai, learned their secret . . . well, that couldn't be helped.
Gareth filled in the last hole she'd dug and tried to stomp the sod
down.

"I'm sorry," she apologized to the spirit of the place for
disturbing it. She spent the rest of the morning writing down
what she had discovered here—and idly wondered if a child of
hers would read it or, if he or she did, believe so wild a story.
Then she packed up her belongings and moved on.

A scattered herd of gray-green antelope was feeding where the
airtruck had been parked. They raised their heads and sat up,
curious, as she passed by, and then returned to eating.

Her intended route led her southeast toward the marshlands,
where she would hunt a shrub whose seeds produced a form of
digitalis. There, too, grew shagbark, for aspirin, and a water lily
whose tubers, when parboiled and allowed to ferment, yielded a
potent anesthetic. She mentally reviewed these and other items,
like a person going shopping.

The farther she walked the less she thought about the strangers. She felt no kinship to them. They probably were the
descendants of the Builders, but they were too fantastic, too
unreal, to be considered comfortably. By the time she reached
home again, if what they said was true, they would have visited
the village, done their tests, and talked to everyone. They might
even have found their way into the cube. That idea intrigued her;
she wondered if they could, and what they might find if they did.
But, since they had the whole world to explore, or so they said,
by the time she returned they'd probably have come and gone
and their visit would be old news.

What mattered more right now was the sweep of clouds
coming in from the sea, another mass piling up inland. If the two
systems met, there would be a thunderstorm.

By midafternoon her head had begun to ache. She stopped to
rest and ate some bread and dried meat, although she wasn't
hungry. The food didn't help the headache. An hour later she
took an aspirin pellet and drank what was for her a lot of water.

Her legs began to ache, and her shoulders felt sore from the pack. When she reached back to adjust it, all her joints hurt and she broke into perspiration from the effort.

Observing these symptoms in anyone but herself, she would have recognized them for what they were. But Gareth was never ill, and it did not occur to her that she was ill now. She dismissed it as fatigue, the aftermath of mental shock, and rather scorned herself for being so affected when she had not consciously realized she was.

Then she considered the people at home. If she was so upset, they must be, too. Perhaps it had been wrong of her to leave them, to come back here again. When people were afraid of something, especially something over which they had no control, they could make themselves very sick—until illness made what frightened them unimportant.

She walked on, her thoughts chasing themselves in circles, her stride slowing with each mile, until a wave of nausea made her stop and quite abruptly lose her lunch. When she wiped her face, she felt the high fever in her skin and knew then she was sick.

For a moment fear blotted out reason. All she could think of was that she was a hundred miles from home, completely alone, in an area where no one ever came. No one would think to look for her for three weeks. Then common sense made her sane again—no one knew where to look. If she was very ill, she'd die. If she wasn't, she'd cure herself and walk home.

She sat down and consulted her map. The drawing blurred and she had to squint to focus. Perhaps two miles away was a spring. If she was going to be sick, she wanted water nearby. She put the map away, struggled to her feet, and plodded on.

The wind blew waves of variegated green over the plain. Animals moved restlessly; some called out warnings to their kind while others raced about like children anticipating a treat. High above, kite lizards slowly wheeled and banked, playing in the updraft.

It took her an hour to walk those two miles. She stopped twice to throw up. She found the spring by sheer luck, nearly falling in the pool after making her way around an outcropping of rocks. There was no kind of shelter, only trees and thorn bushes left untrampled by the animals who came to drink. She forced herself to drink slowly to replace the liquids she had lost, spread her sleeping bag on the rock, crawled in, and curled up into shivering misery.

When the storm came, she was too sick to care and only pulled the flap of the leather bag over her head to keep out the cold water. The pelting rain drummed against her, lightning sheeted from cloud to cloud, and great bolts burned from cloud to ground and back again while thunder cracked and rumbled. The only time she moved was to reach out and clutch the flap the wind tried to blow off her.

By the time the storm moved on, she was unconscious. The wind searched her out and whipped the flap of her bag open to expose her head. A tall blue strider coming to the spring to drink saw her there and started, but since this animal was motionless, the strider paused to sniff her hair, then backed away and sneezed and wiped his muzzle with his forepaws.

Birds came and sat on the sleeping bag, finding it a handy elevation from which to keep a lookout for danger. A family of spotted dabblers, burrowing rodents, investigated this curiosity and chirped to one another about its peculiar scent. They raced back and forth across the bag, leaving small muddy footprints. When one was bold enough to step on her cheek, Gareth twitched, and all the dabblers fled in panic.

The sunset was a theatrical display of clouds and colors. With it, the local herds came to drink. Some shied away at the sight or smell of this thing lying so close to the water. Others challenged it, advancing closer and closer in rushes and feints to frighten it away, or at least preoccupy it while their cohorts drank.

Twilight came. Predators stalked the fringes of the herds and grew more bold with darkness. Packs of scavengers quarreled and snuffled from kill to kill.

In her damp fur-lined cocoon Gareth alternately chilled and sweated and dreamed the twisted dreams of fever. As the night grew colder, she woke at intervals. Nausea came and went in waves, accompanied by anxiety. In her lucid moments all she could think about was home. She wanted to be in her own house, in her own bed, comforted by light and warmth and dry sheets and pillows.

CHAPTER
13

AS SOON AS THEY LEFT GARETH, THEY CALLED COMMANDER Nathan. He listened to their excited report as impassively as he listened to everything, studying them, the cabin around them, his mouth compressed into a noncommittal line, hands clasped atop the little paunch that bulged over his belt. Wesley Hall was in the midst of telling him about the domestic animals when the commander interrupted. "What's your ETA?"

"Twelve minutes, twenty-three seconds, sir," answered Major Singh.

"Are you near the beach?"

"Yes, sir."

"Land there. Wait until I personally give you clearance to proceed. Is that understood?"

"Yes, sir. Is there some problem at the base, sir?" asked the major as he obediently banked right to circle toward the sea. His question was ignored, and the commander did not speak until the airtruck landed on a shingle beach.

"Am I correct in assuming that in your excitement none of you took any precaution against contagion? None of you put on your suits or helmets? That you touched and breathed on these people and they did the same to you?"

From the muffled groans of the others, Lee knew they were experiencing the same sinking feeling as she, the same stab of anxiety at recognition of a serious mistake. Without wanting to, she remembered Nathan's remark about death as a portion of the budget. "Your assumption is correct, Commander," she admitted.

He studied her with hooded eyes, then slowly shook his head as if he didn't want to believe what he knew to be true. "You of all people."

"There may not be a problem," said Major Singh. "We're perfectly healthy. Those people weren't sick."

"Not when you found them," Nathan agreed calmly. "Go back after a few days' incubation time. You entered a human colony today which no outsider has visited in five hundred years. From what you tell me, it's a colony apparently devastated by some old disaster. What if that disaster was biological?"

"We never expected to find people," Lee said in self-defense. "We were so shocked we just didn't think."

"Obviously."

There was silence in the airtruck cabin. Outside, a wave poured against the shingle beach. The tide was coming in.

"Sir? Should we go back and get those people in the compound —bring them in for testing?" Major Singh asked finally.

"No. We don't have the facilities for that. Stay where you are until I get isolation quarters set up for you here. My first responsibility is to my staff," the commander said. "Once we know how you four were affected, we can send a medical field unit out to the colonials."

"There's no guarantee we'll get sick, is there?" asked Tai. "I mean, it's not surety that we've exchanged diseases? We didn't eat their food—or drink their water."

Lee stretched and tried to twist away a pain in her back. "We probably gave them new viruses," she said, "and they returned the favor. I remember Gareth sneezing when she got into the truck."

"I'll get back to you." Commander Nathan reached out to press other buttons on his desk and then paused. "You are to be congratulated on your discovery. It is *very* exciting news." His fingers moved, and the screen went blank.

"He certainly knows how to pour cold water," Tai said.

"Sarcastic old man," Wesley Hall grumbled. Wesley Hall was

two years younger than the commander.

"He's scared." Lee reached over Major Singh's shoulder and pressed the hatch release. "So am I. I'm going for a walk."

The waves washed onto a rocky shore. All around were high cliffs. Disturbed by the airtruck's arrival, the birds wheeled and cried and circled overhead. Lee barely was aware of them.

"What have we done?" she asked herself aloud. "What have we done?" She wasn't sure just what she meant by asking that. It wasn't only her own lack of judgment that she questioned, but the corporation's, or whatever old subsidiary of theirs that had brought a colony here and left it, unrecorded, to get along as best it could, to be blundered into now. Who was responsible?

It was nightfall when Commander Nathan called them home. By that time they were tired and hungry and not in the best of moods. What Tai called "cold water pouring" had had its effect. They had expected to come back triumphant. Instead they were pariahs.

Quarantine was thorough. As the airtruck eased down, a team of pressure-suited personnel ran to surround the vehicle and spray it with disinfectant foam in quantities that billowed up and over the cabin windows.

"From the outside we must look like a gigantic spittle bug nest," Lee commented as they struggled into suits and helmets in the close quarters of the cabin. When allowed to emerge, each was met by a barrage of foam and then led blind into a hastily converted storage building. There they removed their clothes, put them in bags that were in turn put into a vacuum can, and the can was removed so that its contents could be sterilized, while the four went to shower.

The door was secured and locked from the outside, and they could hear the crew spraying the exterior.

Space had been partitioned into four private rooms, a common room with a table, four stools, a terminal, and an autoserve unit for food and drinking water. Cameras monitored the common room and the medical unit next door, where the computer gave each of them an exhaustingly thorough physical.

From the time they emerged from their showers, and on through the evening, they were questioned by Commander Nathan, the science staff, and the administrative staff. It was called debriefing, a term that always amused Lee since such sessions were anything but brief. The first question asked by a fellow scientist was: "By what right were you granted special privileges and thus allowed to make a major discovery?" The second question was: "Having discovered humans, why did you fail to report immediately to the base and, by so failing, put us all in jeopardy?"

The pain in her back crept up to her neck and lodged there. She was sure now it was psychosomatic; if ever anything was a pain in the neck, debriefing sessions were. Before she went to bed at two A.M., she took two aspirin. She fell asleep thinking about the people in that compound, the serenity in their faces that she did not understand. She was wakened in the morning by five explosive sneezes, followed by vigorous nose blowing.

"Bless you," she called softly.

"Thak you." Tai appeared in the doorway to the tiny room. "I thig I have a code." Her eyes were puffy, but other than that she looked normal.

"Sounds that way," Lee agreed, and reached up to open the window shade. Sunlight brightened the room.

Tai's nose wrinkled, and she turned from the glare to sneeze into a handful of tissues. "Sorry," she apologized as she wiped her eyes. "Codes bake be very physical."

"I noticed. How are the men?"

"Restless. They've bid up ad hour ad exhausted all edertaidbed possibilities with breakfast."

Lee grinned at her. She knew Wesley Hall well enough to know how quickly inactivity made him itchy. "But they're not sick?"

"Dot so far. How 'bout you?"

"Well, I feel no pressing urge to get up—but I suspect that's because I know we can't go anywhere today."

The medical computer announced that all four were harboring new microbes that were close relations of ancient Earth strains. It predicted colds and flu and a variety of other, more drastic possibilities, but promised gastrointestinal symptoms could be kept under control by existing medication. "So we won't die of dysentery or embarrassment," Lee said. The computer ignored her and expressed confidence in its ability to develop eventual cures for all problems. Until then they were confined to quarters.

True isolation would have been more easily endured than what the four were subjected to. The presence of cameras and terminals meant they could be watched, talked to, and questioned at will, and they were. The corporate executive staff aboard the *Kekule* joined in by delayed relay after seeing the films Lee and Major Singh had taken.

What began as debriefing evolved into a marathon question-and-answer session. Slowly it began to bother Lee that for all this talk and expressed clinical interest, no one seemed interested in the individual people themselves. Instead the colony was referred to as "it." "*It* must have been a write-off." "*It* was socio-technologically nonviable." "*It* will save us months of research time." There was some discussion as to whether, now that they'd seen pictures of the colonists, there was any point in considering the planet further. "After all, who wants to live in an environment that turns you into a freak? It's hardly a marketable point—regardless of the beautiful scenery."

At noon of the second day Tai went to bed with her cold. By that evening Wesley Hall was sick with fever and stomach problems. Lee and Major Singh, still ambulatory, continued to answer questions. By the end of the third day Lee felt she had been talking forever, that her knees were locked into right angles and her rump was permanently flattened by sitting. Besides all this, she didn't feel well, and she kept thinking of the Mitchell girl out there somewhere alone. Suppose she was sick?

"Commander Nathan," she said as the group broke for dinner, "could we speak with you privately?"

When the last of the staff had left the conference room and he was alone on screen, she explained her worry.

"I'm truly sorry," the commander said, "but until we know what we're dealing with, I don't want any more of my people exposed. We can't bring her back here—"

"We don't have to," Lee said quickly. "I can go out and find her and take her home. Her entire enclave may be ill, may need help."

"I'm going with you," Major Singh said. "I'm going crazy locked up in here."

"We could use the portable medix as we use it when someone's sick or wounded doing field work," Lee went on. "We could do all the basic medical tests without exposing additional personnel. If we need drugs or supplies, they could be air-dropped."

The commander considered this, chewing thoughtfully on the inside of his right cheek. "It's a good idea, except for minor details. Who's going to take care of you two if you collapse? You're both running low-grade fevers now, and you're responding only slightly to medication. You're both vital to my staff—"

"I won't collapse," Lee said firmly. "I don't feel well, but I can do what I have to. I also feel my symptoms are aggravated by boredom."

"Besides," Major Singh added, "all we need is strength enough to crawl to the truck, and the autopilot will carry us back here."

The commander sat studying their faces on his screen, his right hand distractedly massaging his bald spot. The movement of his arm partially obscured his face so that Lee could not read his expression.

"When would you want to leave?" he asked after several minutes had passed.

CHAPTER
14

AFTERWARD GARETH NEVER THOUGHT TO QUESTION HOW they found her—people who could build machines that flew from star to star were obviously capable of doing anything—and so she never knew the hours spent that night searching for one human figure among the thousands of animals grazing and sleeping on the darkened plain.

With landing lights blazing, the would-be rescuers circled the mounds where she had been, hoping to find her departure trail visible as a shadow in the long grass. But any trail she might have left was indistinguishable from that of other animals drifting through the area.

"The last satellite picture of her here was taken eighteen hours ago," Singh said. "How far could she go?"

Lee considered the girl's long stride. "Twenty miles?"

"So if we scan a fifty-mile square, we might pick her up?"

"Unless she's sleeping in a cave."

"Are there caves out here?"

"Who knows?"

He nodded acceptance of that chance, flew to the far edge of the area and switched to computer pilot. In lines as unswerving as an ancient farmer plowing a field, the airtruck began its search.

They took turns watching the screens; one monitored the infrared camera that revealed the land below to be teeming with life forms of all sizes, each form radiating heat energy; the other watched the light-amplifying camera's screen where the plains appeared to be in constant early dawn. It was after two A.M. when the infrared camera picked up an oblong shape atop a colder rock formation.

"Could be!" Singh announced. Lee took control from the computer and circled down to look. "There's water right beside it. Hellova place to sleep if that's her." He set the LA camera on close-up, and Gareth's face emerged from the blue-gray blur. "She looks dead!" he whispered.

"No, I think she's sleeping. As cold as it is, if she had died . . ." Lee didn't finish, remembering his squeamishness about physical details.

"If we put on the landing lights, we might scare her," he said worriedly. "I don't think she's ever seen bright lights."

"I can't land in the dark with all those bushes and that water hole," Lee said, but circled away to keep the worst of the glare from shining on that still face.

When the lights came on, the grassland below exploded into movement. Animals ran in every direction; frightened bleatings and cries rose above the whine of the airfoils. The airtruck had to hover and wait until ground traffic cleared on the field.

When the hatch opened, cold air flooded the cabin. Both Lee and Major Singh shivered as they stepped out into the quiet. The air smelled of grass bruised by the airtruck's landing. Water splashed over rocks. From the distance came an animal's eerie yelping cry, and another answered farther off.

"Creepy, isn't it?" Major Singh whispered.

Lee took a deep breath, glad to be outdoors again.

It seemed to Gareth that statues on the mounds had come to life. They loomed above her, their round heads gleaming like brown bubbles, with vague faces that came and went, their thick bodies covered in shiny cloth. They did a dance around her, bobbing, weaving, coming close to kneel beside her, paying homage. Their hands were almost human, but their touch felt dry-cold, like a lizard's fingers.

She could hear someone breathing in shallow gasps, as if in fear, and then knew it was herself she heard. The statues made murmuring noises. One floated up and out of sight. The other remained kneeling and fumbled at its middle, as if hunting something concealed there.

A hand reached toward her and pressed something cold over her nose and mouth. She tried to turn away. The statue made soothing sounds—the pain in her chest diminished. In relief she stopped struggling and let her eyes fall shut. The sun was very bright. Why was the air so cold?

Dream became nightmare. They put straps around her sleeping bag so she couldn't move. They picked her up and carried her out of the light into darkness, and she believed they had taken her inside a mound and closed the door. She twisted, frantic to escape. The lizard hands touched and tried to hold her.

"I'm sorry!" she cried out. "I'm sorry I dug around your mound! I only wanted to know what you were! Please—I don't want to be trapped inside of stone!"

A bubble head appeared above her, not far from her face. She could hardly see in the dim light, but it was there. It made noises, and then its hands reached up to its neck and it began to lift off its head. She shut her eyes and tried to bury herself within the sleeping bag.

"We're terrifying her," Lee said. "She doesn't know us in the helmets."

"Nathan said to keep them on."

"I know." She dropped her helmet on a seat. "She feels like ice and breathes as if she had pneumonia. She doesn't need more stress. Turn on the translato.—maybe that will help."

"If I can with these gloves . . there we go!"

The translator hesitated and then said, "Self-congratulatory expression."

"We're not at our brightest either." Lee stripped off her gloves and tucked them in her pocket. "It's late, we're tired—"

"And scared," said Major Singh. "Never forget scared. She looks so sick and we're responsible—"

"Gareth?" Lee waited for the translator to repeat each phrase. "Don't be afraid. It's Lee Hamlin and Major Singh. We've come to take you home—leave on the mask." She caught the girl's cold hand. "The mask helps you breathe."

The girl's eyes opened and searched the cabin, but it was impossible to tell if she was conscious. "We've come to help you and take you home." Lee tried to reassure her. A very long moment passed before Gareth turned to look at her and breathed a sigh of relief that ended in an obviously painful cough.

"I'm very sick," she whispered when she could speak. "I think I'm dreaming." Her eyes began to close, and she forced them open. "Where are the other two? Your friends?"

"Back at our base. Asleep. It's late at night."

Gareth appeared to think this over. "That's why it's dark," she concluded and let her eyes fall shut again.

They tried to be as gentle as they could getting her out of her wet sleeping bag and clothing and hooking her up to the medix system. They explained what they were doing and said they hoped she could understand. The cramped cabin made movement awkward, and their nervousness didn't help.

"When one of my crew gets hurt, I just rip their jackets off and shove these instruments in place," Major Singh confided so the translator couldn't hear. "I never think to wonder if the blood test stings or the metal's cold. But look at that arm—there's not a spare ounce of fat. What if we hit something? Like a nerve?"

"We won't," Lee assured him with more confidence than she felt. She was used to working with animals, not people. "And the tissue sample is so small. . . ." She paused, distracted; for all her fragile appearance, the girl's skin was extraordinarily tough.

"Tissue?" he said. "You mean it takes a bite out of us? That sharp sting you feel when—"

"Don't think about it," she whispered. "You've had it done a hundred times and it never bothered you."

"Yes, but I didn't know what it was. The next time I might faint."

She smiled at him, thinking he was joking to put her at ease, and she liked him for it.

"Field Unit One?" The computer's voice was loud in the cabin. "I have no previous data on this patient. Personnel files confirm no crew ID. Please identify and justify."

Lee put on a headset to avoid disturbing the patient while answering the computer's questions. An hour later medication had been given, but she was still talking with the computer and with the medical crew at the base when she glanced over to see the major watching Gareth. On his face was a look of such naked gentleness and longing that it shocked her. My God, she thought, he's going to fall in love with her! She wanted to reach out and touch him and pull him back to safety—but instead she touched the radio button and took off the headset. At the sound of the computer's androgenous and disciplined voice, the man's face resumed its familiar mask.

Gareth woke sweating and thirsty, the sun in her face. Large animals were sleeping on either side of her. She could hear them breathing, one slow and steady, the other softly snoring. She lay quite still, afraid to move, unsure in her groggy state just what to do. If she moved and scared them, they might jump up and step on her in their panic to get away—if they were grazers. If they were hunters, they might bite.

She sniffed, trying to identify by scent, but no scent was familiar. Cautiously, noiselessly, she turned, listened to make sure the breathing hadn't changed, and opened her eyes. She grinned, dopily amused by her idea of sleeping animals. It was almost as funny as seeing Major Singh with a brown glass bubble over his head. She raised up on an elbow. Lee Hamlin slept in a nearby seat, head against the window, hair gleaming in the sun. Gareth stared at the hair and wondered how she had come to be here. Then, tired by this exertion, she lay down again.

She had been very sick! Remembering, she risked a quick breath. It hurt only a little. She tried a slower, deeper breath. The pain and congestion were still there but greatly diminished. She would live. She had dark bruises on both arms and tiny puncture marks: this discovery made her frown—had an animal stepped on her? Bitten her?

Her sleeping bag was gone, and in its place she was covered by a red blanket with letters on it. Her boots were off, gone, like her clothes. She vaguely remembered being touched, talked to, treated as a patient. They had probably saved her life, she thought with a rush of gratitude.

Wanting to ask questions, she turned to Major Singh and considered touching him or coughing, but as she looked she saw he needed a shave and had deep stress lines around his eyes. He snored like a man exhausted. The Hamlin woman looked tired too. Maybe she had been a difficult patient?

A large animal snorted outside the window and brayed a loud yodeling call. Neither stranger stirred. Gareth pushed herself up far enough to look out. They were still beside the water hole.

It was midmorning by the time the two awoke. Between naps of her own, she had learned the landscape of their faces, been relieved to see her pack and sleeping bag lying in the freight bay, counted the seats three times, wondered why these people had come back to look for her, and decided it was probably to ask more questions. She'd imagined what it would be like to have a child that looked like them, and decided she would love it anyhow. Besides, it might take after her side and not the father's. Maybe just being born here would make it look better. Children often altered their faces by assuming the expression of the parent who most influenced their minds.

Lee Hamlin woke first and seemed surprised to be where she was. The bewilderment that crossed the woman's face before full consciousness made Gareth feel more at ease. It was a very human reaction. And then the genuine gladness of both these strangers when they saw that she was feeling better almost made her trust them.

She listened closely as they explained why they were here and why they wore the bubbles. Her first reaction was indignant anger that they could have brought this harm to her, to everyone she knew. Then common sense and pragmatism took over. The thing was done; it was accidental. Anger solved nothing, changed nothing.

"If everybody's sick at home, will your drugs help them?" she asked.

"We think so. You're responding," Lee said.

"You don't look well," Gareth told her bluntly. "Can you cure yourselves? Or can your machine?"

"We think so," the woman said again. She did not promise.

Gareth thought this over. The villagers might not like being treated by these people. But if they were as ill as she had been—and then she thought of Paul and Margo and the others in the compound.

"Please take me home," she begged. "They're going to need help."

"And they'll get it," Major Singh promised, "but not from you, not until you're well. We'll take care of them."

CHAPTER
15

WHEN THEY FLEW OVER THE VILLAGE, ONLY A FEW PEOPLE were working in the fields. The beach was empty. They landed in front of Gareth's door. No one came to meet them but a walla. The only sound was the song of a hen celebrating an egg.

"It's much too quiet. Something's wrong." Gareth slipped free of Major Singh's supportive arm and stood alone, clutching the red blanket around her. "Margo? Paul? Is anybody here?"

The hen quit singing. There was silence. She started down the path to the dome, unsteady but determined. The other two followed. As she neared the door, it opened slowly and Paul emerged, walking with a cane. He stopped short at the sight of her.

"Gareth—why are you dressed like that?"

"It doesn't matter. Are you sick? Is everyone?"

"Oh, yes," he said easily, "everyone here and most of the village."

Lee made a discouraged noise, and the major said something about "work cut out," that Gareth didn't grasp.

"They're blaming it on you," Paul told them.

"How bad is it?"

Paul hesitated. "Two have died in the village." He took a deep breath and leaned against the door. "But we can discuss that later too. You look like the rest of us, Gareth—and your friends don't look much better. Did they take you to their compound?"

"No. They found me at the water hole on the plains." She explained why they had come back for her. "Their medicine saved my life. They came to help the rest of us."

"We must get you to bed," Lee said firmly to Gareth. "I'll get you settled in, and the major can take care of Paul—and then we'll see about the others."

"The villagers may not want your help," Paul warned. "They're afraid as well as sick."

Ten minutes later Gareth was in her own bed, her protests ignored, and left with nothing to do but worry and watch the fire in the fireplace that Lee ignited by pointing a metal cylinder at the logs. Seeing the logs start to smoke and then flame, without a match, was as unreal as the fact that she was safe at home again. The speed and ease with which these people did things left one no time to think, to understand. That bothered her, and she wondered if it ever bothered them—but they seemed so sure of themselves.

Through the window she could hear the muffled voices of Paul, Major Singh, and the translator. They sounded as if they were sitting on the airtruck's ramp. Lee had disappeared, gone to get her a drink of water and not returned. Maybe she's exploring the house, Gareth thought, and wasn't sure she liked that idea. She considered getting up and going to find her, then decided not to; that would imply distrust, and besides, she lacked the energy.

Searching for the kitchen, Lee had found herself instead in what appeared to be a lounging area. Windows looked down across the ruins and beyond, over the trees to the village. Shelves and stacks of books were everywhere, volumes of a type she'd seen only in museums.

Above the bookshelves were portraits of men and women who resembled Gareth in their graceful gauntness. They gazed down at her with clear untroubled eyes or sat in half profile, calmly regarding something in the past. Several appeared to be in uniform, but she couldn't be sure. None were dimensionally precise computer images; they were stylized likenesses hand-painted on wood or cloth-covered boards. All needed cleaning.

The furniture, the fur throws, the cushions—how did they

clean all that? Like Gareth's room this area was heated by a fireplace. Who cut those trees and split them and carried them in here to be burned? Just thinking of the work involved depressed her. If one had to do all this robot labor to exist, there would be time left for nothing else.

What a brutal way to live, and yet . . . she looked up at those faces in the paintings, and thought of Gareth's face and Paul's and the others here. Perhaps because they never knew there was a better way, they could accept this life.

After getting lost several times, she found the room where Gareth had shown them the pump and managed to make the contraption produce water. It gave her an absurd sense of satisfaction to see the liquid spill out and splash into the stone sink. She filled several mugs and set them on a wooden tray she found on a shelf, then rummaged in the cabinets for edibles.

On a platter, covered by a smelly cloth, was cooked meat, the upper portion of an animal's leg, highly redolent of woodsmoke and covered with salt rime, green mold, and tiny seeds. There was also a cheese substance, veined with mold. She sniffed; the thing emitted vile off gases. Wrapped in what appeared to be oiled cloth, but what she suspected was a specially tanned skin, were loaves of bread, their crusts so hard they clicked beneath her fingernails. She recognized them as bread only because they resembled the things Wesley Hall baked after pulverizing the seeds of native grasses.

Wesley might appreciate all this, but she could not bring herself to feed these things to Gareth. Just looking at them made her queasy; the thought of anyone's eating them was revolting. But perhaps that was the only sort of food these people had.

That realization made her sit down at the table, temporarily overcome by culture shock. The medical computer's instructions to "keep the patient warm, comfortable, and adequately nourished" were simple in her world, where all shelter was climate controlled, food available at the press of a button, and laundry done by sonic cleaners that reissued garments sterilized and folded. But in this world, without machines, she suddenly understood that following those simple instructions involved endless work and knowledge—work she lacked the time for and knowledge she had no way of acquiring. To be trapped here forever, powerless . . .

A creaking noise somewhere in the building startled her from her preoccupation. It was so quiet here in this world without motors. She rose, forced back her fear, picked up the tray, and found her way back to Gareth's room. The girl was sleeping peacefully, curled on her side, her arms wrapped around a pillow.

The major was alone when she got back to the truck. "Where's Paul?"

"Went to tell the others about us."

"How sick is he?"

"He has the flu. Not bad. Not good." He grunted as he lifted the medix onto an equipment cart. "I don't think I've got the energy to lug that thing from door to door," he said apologetically. Sunlight winked off his helmet as he turned to her. "Maybe you should put your helmet on? As much for the added oxygen as for germs? You look a little—uh—"

"I feel that way, too," she admitted. "It occurred to me in there that we may have bitten off more than we can chew. And I got scared."

At that he glanced away to watch an insect hovering over a flower. "Yeah," he said. "There's a lot of that going around." His eyes met hers again. "How's Gareth?"

"Sleeping. I'm going to heat some soup and leave a thermos mug of it on her bed table in case she wakes up hungry. Would you like some?"

"I don't think so, thanks."

"We haven't eaten since last night. We won't be much help here if we faint a lot."

He grinned and nodded. "O.K., but something without too much flavor?"

Birds came to watch them drink their soup, fear of the motor's noise apparently forgotten. Drab, long-legged, and beady-eyed, the birds stalked about with a proprietary air. A walla came and chased the birds, more from habit than animosity, for it made no attempt to catch them. The sun was warm. Lee leaned against the airtruck. Major Singh sat staring into space, his eyes half shut. The urge to nap was tempting. When Lee started yawning, she got up and put her helmet on.

"We can't put it off any longer, can we?" The major sighed as he reached for his helmet.

The cart left neat wheel tracks on the path down to the dome. To enter there was like walking into a bizarre greenhouse. A-frame wooden racks stretched in rows, the racks festooned with yarn, cloth, and hides in various stages of dyeing or drying. An antique lab table was littered with dye pots. A half-finished carpet folded from a wooden loom. Around the dome's inner rim flowers grew in tubs and spilled from hanging baskets, adding their smells to the mixture of craft and household odors. Lee quickly adjusted her helmet so that she breathed only pure air.

"Hello?" she called. "Is anybody here?" The translator repeated the question. "If you're in bed, don't get up, just answer so we can find you."

No one answered, but in a moment Margo appeared in an aisle between the racks. "You look more like insects than medics," the old woman said, referring, Lee hoped, to their helmets.

"How are you?"

"I've felt better. Paul's gone to tell the village about you. I wish he hadn't, but there's no one else to go."

Their living quarters were partitioned off by bookshelves and cupboards and centered beneath a hanging light panel with a power cell still functioning. There was a sink and heating unit, both original equipment and still working. Once the major saw these things, he wanted to explore the entire dome and see what else still worked and why.

"*Why* is because our family never moved anything," Margo

said as she submitted to Lee's medix check. "We always lived in here and we always let well enough alone. Not like most people—moving walls and breaking old things. The AIRD house now—they had light until two years ago when Uri decided to shingle the roof instead of just patching up the leak."

Lee glanced at the major to see if he was getting the same impression she was—that these people were descended from scientists who first worked in this laboratory. From what Gareth said, each household was responsible for keeping certain knowledge alive. Who better than a biochemist would know how to extract fiber from plants, or dyes, or tanning agents, and oils? Wesley Hall could, she thought, and if she was forced to exist that way, she supposed she could remember practical applications of her education.

The major was on his knees, studying a narrow channel in the worn floor, preoccupied by his own interests. "Are there lights in the village?" he asked.

"No." Margo shook her head. "That's much newer than the compound. The Builders had no hand in it. Why are you wearing those bowls over your heads?"

"To keep from giving you more germs," Lee said.

"Or getting them?" asked Margo slyly.

"That too."

"How does this work?" She pointed to the medix. As Lee attempted to explain, Margo hunched over to listen, her eyes darting from dial to dial. "It can think? It can understand?"

"It can analyze, yes, and discriminate. Within the limits of its stored data—"

"You don't want to admit it thinks?" Margo persisted.

"It doesn't think as humans do," Lee said.

"Smarter?"

"In many ways. But it has limitations."

"So do I. Does it have a name?"

"No. It's a . . . machine."

"I know that. But it still has a spirit. My loom has a spirit of its own. Some days it wants to work; other days it likes to be quiet and think."

Later, when they were outside again, on their way to the next building, Lee commented, "What an odd mixture of intelligence and superstition Margo is."

"Because of what she said about the loom?" he asked, and when Lee nodded, "That's not odd. Every machine I've ever seen had a spirit all its own. Some like damp climates, some like dry. They'll take a dislike to someone and refuse to work for them." He matched her stare for stare. "It's true, Dr. Hamlin. Besides, Margo was talking to keep from thinking. I'd be scared if I were they and we arrived . . . even before this happened. Someone lives here . . . at least I think they do." They knocked on the plank door.

By late afternoon their cart tracks veered from one side of the path to the other, and the two volunteer medics were tired. It was one thing, they had learned, to be moderately ill when all they had to do was sit and talk, but quite another to feel that way and try to work, especially in a situation where everything was strange. Both were puffing as they pushed the cart up the slope to the airtruck.

"If we're this tired after fifteen people, how are we going to help the village?" Major Singh wondered aloud.

"Very slowly," said Lee, "and that's if they cooperate. If they're hostile—"

"Don't think about it." The major opened the hatch, sat down to rest, and patted the floor as an invitation for her to join him.

"I want to check on Gareth first," she said.

"Afraid if you sit down you won't get up?"

"Sure of it."

"Don't forget the translator."

From her window Gareth had watched them leave Uri's house and go back to the airtruck. They staggered with exhaustion. When a cart wheel jammed against a rock in the path, both bent to free it, and their bubbled heads cracked together. They had to grab each other's arms to keep from falling. Although she wanted to laugh, that had touched her. No matter what else she might think of them, there was no denying their good qualities. She might even like them if she got to know them.

Since she'd been awake, she'd bathed and washed her hair, gone down to the kitchen and gotten some ham, cheese, and bread—and had time to think. She really couldn't blame them for what had happened—even though she wanted to. How would they know?

At the sound of footsteps on the ramp she got back in bed and pulled the comforter up, playing the good patient. The woman paused in the doorway and asked shyly, "Are you awake?"

"I'm almost well. How are the others?"

"They'll recover." At the sight of the plate with the remains of Gareth's snack, a strange expression came over Lee's face, as if she wanted to gag. She sat on the edge of the nearest chair.

"Are you sick? Can I help?" Gareth asked.

"I'm fine," she lied. "Just tired." She looked at her through the bubble. "You certainly recovered fast."

"Sleep," Gareth said. "And your care. I drank all the medicine you left. It tasted terrible, but it gave me lots of strength."

"Medicine?"

Gareth lifted the soup thermos.

"Oh. Yes. That helped?"

"It was very beneficial." Gareth wondered at the woman's smile. She didn't think she'd said anything amusing. "Paul told me you were going to the village tomorrow. I'm going with you."

"No, you're not."

"I have to. Besides, you might get hurt if you go alone."

"But they know we want to help them."

"How can they *know* that?" Gareth said. "Being told and believing are two different things. You need me with you."

"You're just getting over pneumonia and—"

"I wanted to talk to you about that—would you please write me your recipe for making the medicine that cures pneumonia?"

"The computer could . . . I suppose." Lee sounded as if she didn't quite approve of the idea. "Is there anything I can get you before I go?"

"You're going home?"

"No. We're staying here tonight in case we're needed."

"That's kind of you."

"No, it's not," the woman said and left quickly, as if uncomfortable with gratitude—or with me, Gareth thought. But then, they didn't have much in common.

Major Singh was talking to the base when Lee returned to the truck. On the screen the commander's office looked so new and clean and comfortably barren. The commander appeared to have gained weight since she'd seen him last—or was it only in contrast to the slenderness she'd seen all day? He looked so . . . sturdy.

"How are you, Dr. Hamlin?" the commander asked in greeting. "You look a little ragged. I was just telling the major, we're going to send you help. We've been monitoring your medix. If the rest of those people are as sick as the first fifteen, there's no way you two can handle the situation alone."

"What made the executive staff change its mind?"

"Simple economics. Since we're going to have to research these colonists, and time for that wasn't budgeted, we can give them medical care at the same time we get the information we need. Everyone volunteered."

"They'll be in isolation gear?" asked Major Singh.

"They could walk on a moon. I don't want anyone else in sick bay."

"How are Tai and Wesley Hall?" Lee asked.

"Better. Bored. Now, what sort of equipment will our people need to do any good?"

They discussed supplies and logistics until Nathan was interrupted by a call from the *Kekule*. "If we need more information, we'll get back to you," he said to Lee and the major. "Where are you sleeping?"

"In the truck."

There was silence in the cabin after the screen went off. The sun had slipped behind the wall, and the compound was deep in shade.

"Management seems to feel these people are just another research project to be fitted into the schedule," Lee said with some bitterness.

"It's a business," the major said quietly. "To you, it's your animals, and to me it's doing my job the best I can with the bonus of seeing new worlds. But we both came into space because we're working for a corporation—and they call the shots. Research and development is very expensive. Each day here is cost-accounted. They're in it for the money. If I really hate what they do, I can always quit and go build toilets in Topeka."

Her irritation dissolved in a laugh. "You have a very pragmatic mind, Major," she said. "You put things into perspective with exquisite logic."

"We engineers are like that," he said as he shifted into the pilot's seat. "Want to fly down to the beach for dinner and a swim?"

CHAPTER 16

"YOUR ATTENTION, PLEASE! YOUR ATTENTION, PLEASE. IF YOU are sick, report to the medical tent for treatment. We're here to help you."

The cube's talking again, Gareth thought as the noise woke her from a dream. It's awfully loud this time.

"If you are sick, report to the medical tent for treatment. We're here to help you," the voice repeated.

With a shock at understanding what the cube was saying, she sat up and looked out the window. It was early morning; the shadow of the woods stretched halfway across the fields. In the courtyard below, the airtruck roof was pebbled with dew.

The cube wasn't turning, but something was happening in the village. A flock of yellow airtrucks was clustered on the road to the beach. In the pasture between the trucks and the first houses stood a dome that glistened in the sunshine. People dressed in silver-gray were hurrying back and forth between dome and airtrucks. Down by the beach were eight tiny yellow domes.

"Please cooperate," the translator's voice ordered. "We don't want to be forced to go from building to building looking for you." There was a series of crackling sounds, and the voice suddenly sounded much more human. "Get back in the trucks!" it shouted. "These primitives are throwing rocks!"

There was a sharp hiss below. The airtruck quivered and then lifted up, so close and fast that Gareth ducked back from the window, frightened. Dew from its roof slapped the glass like rain as it shot away, its jet wash whipping the treetops into frenzy.

She watched it cross the fields and land beside its own kind, and then she got up and began to dress. *Primitives?*

By the time she was halfway to the village, she was sweating from exertion, but that couldn't be helped. There had been no more loud-voiced announcements. One airtruck had flown low over the houses and landed again, leaving a trail of fog. After that there had been sporadic shouting, but it hadn't sounded like villagers. The closer she got, the more medicinal the air smelled.

The row of airtrucks blocked her view. They looked alike, completely identical except for the numbers painted on their sides. She found that fascinating and decided they'd been made from molds. Handmade things were always individual. She walked along the row until she came to the one in which Major Singh and Lee Hamlin had landed. Its hatch was open, and they were gone. As she walked around the truck, she got her first close view of the new arrivals and stopped still and stared.

They could be statues on the mounds! They were short; none was taller than Lee Hamlin. All wore bubbles on their heads and were encased from head to toe in silver suits. Even their hands and boots were silver. Around their waists were bulky belts. Some had silver packs on their backs. They looked as identical as the airtrucks or a hive of insects.

She knew they were human, but they didn't look it, and she thought that if they frightened her they must terrify the villagers. A pair came trotting down the street carrying a man on a stretcher. His legs hung over one end, and his heels plowed twin furrows in the dust. They took him into the silver domed tent.

Several people were lying on the street. Ula Buri was huddled in her open doorway, slumped against the frame, one hand over her face, A pair of silver-suits came around the corner of the house, saw Ula, tumbled her onto the stretcher, and lugged her off to the tent. Gareth felt a rising panic; Paul had said the villagers were sick, but she hadn't imagined it was this bad. She ran to the tent, worry outweighing her fear.

"We've got a walk-in!"

"Watch it! It's not even groggy!"

"Hey, it looks familiar."

"They all look the same."

"Take the stretcher case first."

The medical tent's interior suggested the field hospital of a disaster area. On every side tranquilized villagers lay on air mattresses. Some were having strange reactions to the drug: facial muscles twitched, legs jerked, arms trembled uncontrollably. Space-garbed figures with medix units worked their way among them. One team met incoming patients at the door to measure and weigh them on a sling scale. Gareth watched them rip the sleeve of Ula's tunic, spray her arm with foam, wipe it off and press a tool of some sort against the bare brown skin. The tool left a bruise like the one on Gareth's arm.

"Put her in Row C for medix check."

The helmets and translators made it hard to tell who was talking. Ula's stretcher was unhooked from the scale and carried over to a row of people next to the tent wall. They slid her off the stretcher like a sausage.

"You're next." A gray pudgy hand clasped Gareth's wrist and pulled her toward the scale. "Don't be scared. We're going to make you all better."

Her reaction was pure reflex. She twisted free, struck two quick chopping blows to the bubble, then a third to the silver chest. She was aiming for the midriff, but the height threw her off. From the bubble came a guttural "Oough," and the person sank to its knees, gasping for breath.

In the quiet a voice said, "Gawd! I told you to be careful of that one. Now—"

"Don't stun her! Don't you dare!"

Major Singh shoved his way past two men to stand beside her, to her great relief. Other silver-suits came running. "That's Gareth!" said Lee Hamlin's voice, and then Gareth saw her. "What are you trying to do? She's already had her shots."

"We're trying to inoculate fifteen hundred people in the

shortest possible time, and every damned one is hostile,"
someone answered.

"They're scared to death," said Major Singh. "How would you
like it if a bunch of cloned aliens landed outside your door and
decided to examine you? You'd wet your pants."

"We're not aliens!"

"We look like aliens to them! Use your head!"

"If they're that stupid—"

"Hold it!" A silver-suit raised its arm for quiet. "This is wasting
time. You two take Barry out and make sure he's O.K. Now,
Major Singh, I can appreciate your concern, but I'm in charge
here. We have no time to waste on empathy or culture shock or
dignity. There's too much to do and too few of us to do it. Perhaps
our initial approach was crude, but we're all amateurs at this and
we're doing the best we can."

"Dr. Stein." Lee Hamlin spoke. "Now that Gareth's here, why
don't we have her talk to the village on the P.A. system? Explain
what we're doing and why—in basic terms. She's their medic.
They'll trust her."

"They might if he hadn't put 'em all to sleep by spraying," the
major interjected.

"That wears off in an hour."

"Why isn't she affected?"

"Wind drift blew the mist away before she got here, probably.
She lives over in the forest," Singh explained, "in the old
administration compound."

"Oh. This is your initial contact? I saw your tapes of her."

They were looking up at Gareth with new interest, some of the
fear and dislike gone from their faces, replaced by a mild
amusement she didn't understand.

"Would she be willing to cooperate—talk to them?" Dr. Stein
asked Lee, as if Gareth couldn't hear.

"Ask her. She's quite intelligent."

"I'm sure . . . you ask her. I'd hate to have her hit me."

"Then don't treat me as if I were simple," Gareth said, and

several people laughed nervously at the translation.

"Let's step outside?" The major pointed to four stretchers waiting to be brought in. "We're holding up production here."

"But what are you doing to people?" Gareth asked. "Are they all this sick? Are they dying? Flu doesn't make you twitch."

"We'll explain," Lee assured her, and led her around the little crowd and out into the sunshine. "When the villagers threw rocks, our people sprayed a chemical in the air that temporarily puts people to sleep. With our helmets on we're not affected—"

"You have no right to do that! Who do you think you are?"

"Our people were afraid someone would get hurt."

"Why didn't you wait for me? I told you I'd go with you—that everyone would be afraid. Why didn't you tell us you were bringing all these strangers here? We could have warned people then."

"We were going to tell you," Lee said. "We didn't know they'd get here so early."

Gareth wasn't sure she believed that. She suspected they hadn't wanted her around to see how they treated people. They were acting as if they were embarrassed by her presence.

"What are they doing in there?"

"Giving people shots for flu and colds and pneumonia. And examining them to determine their general condition," Lee said. "It looks bad, I know, but they're giving them the same medication we gave you. Now what we'd like you to do to help—" She explained about the public address system.

Gareth thought it over. "I won't talk to them on your loudspeaker." The word had only literal meaning for her. "That will just scare them more—and make them afraid of me. They'll think it's the cube talking. I did. So did everybody in the compound. They all came outside to listen, sick as they are. They tried to stop me from coming here. . . ."

Her attention was distracted by a child coming along the street, his legs so unsteady that he had to stop every few feet and hang onto the nearest wall or tree. "Joel," she called, recognizing

him. "Stay there! I'm coming! If you two really want to help, get
your medical machine and come with me."

Gareth didn't wait to see what they decided. She didn't much
care. By the time she reached the little boy, he was sitting on the
grass, frightened and fussing.

"Everyone's sleeping," he told her. "I can't wake them up."

"I know. They'll wake up soon. Don't worry."

"They were sick and now they're sleeping." He pointed to the
dome. "What is that?"

"People have come to help us. Now let's get you home." She
brushed his hair back from his eyes. His forehead was hot and
dry, his eyes too bright.

"They don't look like people, Gareth."

"They're wearing silly clothes. Up we go!" When she lifted
him, she realized how weak she was. The effort made her head
pound, and she had to brace herself against a tree to shift his
weight onto her hip so she could carry him.

"Can I help?" called Major Singh. Joel's arms tightened, and
he tried to bury his face in her hair so hard that she couldn't turn
her head but had to turn her whole body to see the major and
Lee Hamlin, pushing the same cart they'd used the day before,
only now it had more equipment on it.

"I'm scared, Gareth." It was a pleading little moan in her left
ear.

"You're safe," she assured Joel. "Don't squeeze so tight. You're
choking me."

"Let me carry him," Major Singh said.

"No!" The boy wailed and clutched convulsively.

"I'll take him. He lives there." Gareth nodded in the direction
of his house and started walking, knowing if she didn't get there
soon his struggling weight would exhaust her. The other two
followed.

In the yard chickens either lay bedraggled or stumbled about,
clucking with concern. A pig woke and jumped up as if late for an
appointment, took a step and staggered, falling on its rump. It sat

there, pale eyes squinting, trying to understand. A red glider lay
in the middle of the street—Gareth thought it was dead—as was
a walla lying with its lips flexed back, exposing all its teeth. It was
no wonder the little boy was frightened. She was frightened too,
and angry.

She looked back at the other two, ready to accuse, and saw Lee
Hamlin stop to pick up a limp seabird and cradle it in her gloved
hands. After studying it a moment, the woman reached for a tube
on the equipment cart. Gareth heard a hiss of air. Almost at once
the bird struggled back to life and was put down gently on the
ground.

"She made the bird well again," the boy whispered, intrigued.

Lee looked up and saw them watching. "I just wanted to know
if they'd recover. I didn't mean to waste time," she apologized.

Gareth shook her head; she didn't understand these people.

It was dark in Joel's house; the shutters were all closed, the fire
cold ashes. His mother lay curled in bed; his father had collapsed
in a chair and was breathing raggedly. Gareth sat the boy on the
bed and went to open the shutters. Lee Hamlin and Major Singh
stood just in the front doorway, as if afraid to enter.

"We'd better treat the man first, before he wakes up," Major
Singh decided. "He looks pretty powerful."

"He is." Gareth suddenly understood their fear. If this man
woke and saw these creatures standing over him, he might go
into shock and die—or attack them. If he attacked, they would
have to defend themselves. She had no doubt that they could.
And it would all be for nothing.

"You're right," she said. "I'll have to try to talk to people over
your loudspeaker. If they believe me, it will save a lot of grief. If
they don't—"

"It's worth a try," said Lee. "We'll use the speaker in our
truck. But since we're here, let's take care of these three. That
will give the village time to wake up."

Gareth helped as best as she could, but there wasn't much she
could do. She knew nothing of their kind of medicine, and since

the machine did it all, there was little she could learn. As they worked over the boy's father, she started a fire in the kitchen hearth and put a pot of water on to heat for tea. The house was cold. Joel asked endless questions, and they answered patiently. Soon it was obvious the boy was over the worst of his fear. If you didn't see them, she thought, and if it wasn't for the translator, the conversation would sound like normal people talking to a child.

When they left the house almost an hour later, the adults were both sleeping comfortably in bed and Joel was drinking a mug of what they told him was soup but Gareth thought was medicine. The boy appeared to like it.

The streets were still deserted of all but silver-suits, but she could see people moving inside some of the houses. Gareth knocked on several doors. No one answered, and when she tried to open the doors, she could not.

"Gareth," Major Singh said thoughtfully, "I saw what I think were firearms in that boy's house—guns. Why don't they shoot at us instead of throwing rocks?"

She stared at him. "They might kill somebody."

It was his turn to stare.

"We don't shoot at people. Guns are for killing," she explained. "For meat—or marauding animals."

"Oh . . . I'm glad to hear that."

"Do you think we're *that* primitive?"

"I just wanted to make sure."

"Not to change the subject, but would it help if we tried music? Would that lure people outside to listen? I've used it as a lure on field trips. . . ." Lee's voice trailed off.

"Do you have a guitar with you?" asked Gareth, interested. It hadn't occurred to her to ask them about music.

"No. No guitar. But we can provide guitar music. Do you like that?"

"Very much. I play sometimes late at night when I can't sleep."

"You have a guitar?" the major said. "And it still works? After all these years?"

"My grandmother made it. It's silkwood with an ebony neck and tuning keys."

"Wood? It's made of *wood*?"

"Of course . . ." At first she was puzzled, then guessed, "Are your guitars machines?"

"No, but—well, they're . . . Yes," he admitted finally. "That's what you'd call them. They have a power cell and amplifiers and automatic chords—What's so funny?"

She wasn't sure, but she didn't stop laughing until they reached the airtruck.

C H A P T E R
17

INSTEAD OF GUITAR, LEE CHOSE A RECORDING OF SONATAS FOR koto and flute, feeling the ancient elegance of the music might be effective here. As the pure and separate notes drifted out over the village, even the crew stopped to listen. Two minutes passed, then five. Doors opened cautiously. Ten minutes brought a few people outside and many to their windows.

Gareth listened so intently she scarcely seemed to breathe and, when the music ended, had to be reminded of what she'd come here for. "Just talk to them," they told her. "Tell them what they need to know to make them accept our help." After a few shy starts she did so—so well that a line slowly formed outside the tent and a small group gathered where she stood talking beside the airtruck.

"They say most of their families are too sick to walk," she told Lee. "We'll have to go from house to house."

"Will they allow it?"

"Most of them—but some only if I come along."

It was a long morning. People who had traveled light years met people who had never been more than five miles from home. People dressed in suits made of raw material that came from gas clouds in space hurried in and out of houses built of stone and logs.

Margo had said the village was newer than the compound. To Lee it looked much older. Most of the row houses had three rooms with a fireplace at the central core. For the rest of her life

she wouldn't be able to smell ham without thinking of those
kitchens. Hams hung from every rafter, along with bunches of
dried fruit, onions, and strips of jerky.

As in Gareth's house, all furnishings were of wood, dark with
age and use. There were furs and braided rugs for color and
comfort, but these were, to Lee's eyes, filthy. She thought a
bacteria count on the bedding alone would cause medix a mental
breakdown. No animal but man would tolerate a den so dirty.

Sanitation facilities consisted of backyard privies with slab
seats. Each house had a wooden pump mounted over a stone
sink. A spring-fed reservoir on an upper slope gravity-fed water
and was supplemented by cisterns to collect rain and more
bacteria. There was no lighting system; their lamps burned oil
crushed from some native seed or plant.

The villagers were not as tall as the compound dwellers, but
they looked bigger. For whereas the members of Gareth's group
were slim, years of hard manual labor had given the villagers
muscle, and, with their enlarged chest cavities, they looked more
imposing. Exposure to the sun made their skins dark and
leathery. The inoc guns had to be set at maximum to penetrate,
and then they left a bruise, as if diffusion and absorption were
slow or incomplete.

Gareth took all this for granted, but at times Lee and Major
Singh had to make an effort to conceal their revulsion—not
always successfully—at the things they saw. A madman lay
strapped to a bed, filthy, babbling to himself. His eyes looked
odd, and when Lee checked she found his irises brightly ringed
with copper. They saw harelips, hands with missing fingers, a
clubfoot, teeth rotted to the gumline—all this never would have
been allowed to happen in their world. The medix reported so
many stomach ulcers that they stopped to have the unit checked,
thinking it defective. It was not.

By midday Gareth was exhausted. They flew her over to the
compound and convinced her to go back to bed. "What help will

you be if you get sick again?" Major Singh asked bluntly. "You're their only medic. They can spare you now, but not after we're gone."

If the morning seemed long, the afternoon seemed endless. Lee and the major found that without Gareth to vouch for them, some villagers were hostile to them and all were ill at ease. Precious time and energy had to be spent coaxing and cajoling —and in two cases, stunning patients.

"What are we doing here?" Lee asked the major after narrowly missing being clubbed by a chair when they walked into a house uninvited.

"Trying to make up for past mistakes," he said. "The question is, how far past?"

"It's a little late to ask that," she said.

While a temporary camp was set up for the other volunteers, Lee and Major Singh couldn't stay there. Without their helmets they were contagious to their colleagues. They spent a second night sleeping in their airtruck. Both of them felt ill and tired to the bone. "It's depression," she told him. "We couldn't feel this lousy if we were really sick. We'd be dead." Medix gave them more shots and recommended rest. There was no time.

The third day Lee woke up so stiff and sore she could hardly move. Major Singh was little better. When medix reported their condition to control, Commander Nathan called to order them to stay exactly where they were, seated dispiritedly in their airtruck outside Gareth's door. Two hours later an airtruck arrived and landed long enough to drop off Tai, Wesley Hall, and supplies. Lee didn't realize how sick she was until Tai said, "We've come to take care of you," and she felt so grateful that her eyes filled with maudlin tears.

"We can't take you back to the base because all the help is here—you'd contaminate everything. But we can make you comfortable," Wesley Hall assured them. "Don't blubber, Lee. You can't blow your nose with a helmet on."

On the green beside the pool, they lasered down some trees
and in the clearing inflated a dome tent for themselves and one
for each of their patients. The trees provided shade; the gurgling
pipe became a sound screen. "That's the best we can do where
privacy's concerned," Tai said apologetically as she helped Lee
settle in. "Now go to sleep. We'll take care of things."

"What if you get sick again?" Lee wondered.

"We won't. We're immunized against every bug medix found
these past three days. Besides, I refuse to catch anything else.
We don't have time. When you and Singh are up again, Nathan
wants us to check out the MMT, see if we can get inside, and—"

"Why us? We won't know what we're seeing," Lee complained
irritably. "Why not send astrophysicists?"

"They refuse to leave the ship. Their employment contract
says they don't have to. You know how some ship people
are—agoraphobic."

"There are five corporate executives down here now," Lee
said, and when Tai looked surprised, she added, "They came
yesterday—with bodyguards. You didn't know?"

"No . . . why don't they . . . unless we're guinea pigs. We're
the only ones in our group who caught anything. . . ." She stood
beside Lee's cot, frowning to herself, then brightened. "Well, if
we have to, it might be interesting to be the first people in that
place in centuries. And Nathan also wants us to go through their
oldest books to see if they tell us what happened here."

"What other projects does he plan for us?" Lee grumbled,
huddling under the blanket, trying to get warm.

"First, you get well," Tai said as she stooped to leave the tent.
"We'll worry about the rest afterward."

Alone for the first time in days, Lee lay listening to her breath
whisper through the mask that had replaced her helmet. Outside
Tai and Wesley Hall were talking as they opened supply crates.
An airtruck came, unloaded something, and left. An insect
landed with a clicking sound atop her tent. Lee watched its

shadow walk down the yellow plastic, saw it begin to lose its grip and slide away into lazy flight. Her eyes ached, and she closed them. The fountain burbled.

By the following morning sleep had restored her to the point of restlessness. She didn't feel well enough to get up, just well enough to resent being in bed with nothing to occupy her mind. When Tai came in to give her a shot and soup for breakfast, she asked her to ask Gareth's permission to read some of her books. "That way I can pass the time and get some research done, too," she reasoned.

"Would it be so bad if you simply rested?"

"But then I think . . ." She didn't finish the sentence.

"Oh, well, we must avoid that!" Tai said in mock dismay. Several hours later she and Wesley Hall arrived with a dolly load of volumes and a translator with earphones.

"Some are Gareth's, some are Paul's, and some are other people's," Tai said as they began stacking books on the tent floor. "We've debugged them a bit—that's what took so long. Please keep them in order or we'll never remember which belongs to whom. Except Margo—hers are the cloth covers. She says be careful with them. Gareth says she'll look for more when she has time."

Lee was used to books printed on thin film, volumes weighing an ounce or two, small, luxurious bibelots of her computerized world. But these books, their pages made of strange thick paper, sewn together and bound with hide or wooden slabs, weighed more than a pound apiece. She grunted in surprise as she lifted the first one and rested it on her midriff.

It was handwritten in pale ink. "Basic Principles of Identifying and Recovering Xilan Sulphides and Carbonates for Metal Manufacture, transcribed by Dunton Cary, Xilan year 51, in his own hand," read the title page. What followed appeared to be a combined geology and mining text, in very simple language.

As she leafed through, phonetically reading random paragraphs into the translator and studying diagrams and sketches, the concerned tone of the writer became apparent and touched her. Here was a man of advanced technology desperately trying to record the practical applications of what he knew so that his knowledge would survive him and benefit others. That he was at the time of writing old or ill was evident by his handwriting and the spidery tracings of his maps. That the colony was already in deep trouble was plain from his descriptions of manual procedures: sketches of how to shore up an open pit with logs, how to provide ventilation in tunnels, how to build a crusher and a smelter, how to build casts and open them.

By the time she put the book aside and reached for another, Lee found herself wishing Dunton Cary had had a happier life and wondered why she felt he had not. She found part of the answer to that question three texts later in the form of a cookbook illustrated with excellent drawings of native plants and animals. These things, the preface said, could be eaten, "now that it's necessary, without fatal or undue discomfort." Her favorite paragraph began: "Avoid the spotted grazer when in rut as both male and female are revolting. At other times you can walk up and club them." Although the book had lost its title page, she became as fond of its anonymous author as she was of Dunton Cary. She put it aside for Wesley Hall to see.

She brightened with hope when she found a diary, only to learn that it recorded a man's displeasure with everyone he knew. His sporadic entries were made to express venom or to mark his victory over someone. "I burned John's boots today. That will teach him not to trick me," was a typical notation. The diary ended in mid-book with an entry in a feminine hand. "Jack fell off White Cliff today, birding. Broke his neck."

"Served him right," Lee muttered, and picked up the next book.

Throughout that day and the next she read and slept and thought. Sometimes at night Major Singh's coughing woke her, and she would tense with worry until more comfortable sounds returned to the tent across the way. When he was still again, the insects would resume their songs, and she would turn on her cot lamp and read herself back to sleep.

By the end of the second day she needed to rely far less on the translator. The archaic words and spellings had become familiar, especially in the texts. Slang and colloquialisms made the personal journals more difficult to read, but she enjoyed them more. She had started on the books impatient to learn definite information, but as the hours passed she found herself reading for the fun of it. The present and its urgencies receded, and she would glance up from an account of a good beet harvest three hundred years before and be surprised to see her tent walls and remember where she was and what it was she searched for.

Recorded in the diaries were lives of hard work and, to her, very little reward or excitement, and yet there was a sense of peace and time and self-assurance she herself had never known. "Butchered two hogs today," a diary would note. "Fine meat and sausage. The weather held off, but the ocean looks so green you know it's going to rain. Gave a fresh ham to Ula to pay her back for bread. She didn't want to take it. It's hard to stay even with that woman. When her birthday comes around, we'll make her a barbecue." Lee finished the whole diary just to hear how Ula's party went.

Along with the writer of another diary she grieved at the entry. "Our baby died today. I don't know why. Children die so easily—just slip away."

Was that part of the problem, she wondered—high infant mortality? But from what cause or causes? She couldn't remember seeing any pregnant women here. For that matter, what did they feed babies? These women were so thin. The more she read, the less she knew and the more questions arose to be answered.

Footsteps crunched on gravel, then brushed through dry grass behind her tent. Other feet followed, quick and light with claws. It was almost nightfall.

"Major?" That was Gareth's voice. "Aren't you supposed to

be in bed? They told me you were ill."

"I'm O.K." He sounded terrible. "How do you feel?"

"Much better, thank you. . . . I was going to shut the gate."

"I already did that. That little patch of roadway there—it looks like it's original surfacing."

"It is," she said. "The Builders made it."

"It lasts that long?" He sounded pleased.

"Only in that sheltered place. It ends where the creek washed through it, at the log bridge, but you can still see where it led because the trees are twisted and diseased."

"We put an acid in the soil to kill off seeds and spores," he said. "If you don't, on some worlds, tree sprouts and mushrooms poke up overnight—push holes right through the surface. You come out in the morning and you'll see a pound of road balanced atop a half ounce mushroom. The mushrooms cut the chunk off clean. If I could figure out a system that efficient . . ." His hoarse voice trailed off. "Where did the road go if the village wasn't there yet when it was built?"

"To the cube."

"Cube? You mean the MMT," he said. "Then where was the village originally?"

"Right outside the walls—where the woods are now. The trees grow out of hillocks. Shouldn't you be in bed?"

Major Singh said something Lee couldn't hear over the fountain's noise.

There was quiet and the sound of birds settling down for the night. From the other end of the compound came an irate pig squeal and snorting.

"Why do you care about the road?" Gareth asked. Lee got the impression the girl was making an effort to be polite.

"I've built roads like that on every world I've walked on. Including this one. It's part of the job when you make a base."

"How many worlds is that?"

"Seven. Counting Earth. Most aren't worth a landing. When we leave, I always look down from the shuttle, and there's my road, like a signature. You can see them for a long way up."

"That sounds like the music Lee Hamlin told the truck to play to the villagers," Gareth said after a moment.

"Didn't you like that music? People came out to listen."

"It was very beautiful," Gareth said, "haunting . . ."

"Would you like to hear more?"

"No," she answered quickly, and then, as if in apology for her abruptness, "I think your music is like your soup—it's full of energy, very highly concentrated, nourishing—but a taste that would take us some time to get used to."

Singh laughed. "You don't like our soup either? Do you like us?"

There was a pause and Lee found herself almost as interested in the answer as she imagined the major to be.

"There's a ring around the moon tonight," said Gareth. "That means it's going to rain."

CHAPTER 18

"THE ANSWER ISN'T IN THE BOOKS," LEE SAID, "NOT THE ONES I've read."

"I didn't think it would be," Tai said, "or Gareth wouldn't have grown up hearing myths about builders."

"They probably relied totally on computers just as we do," Wesley Hall reasoned. "When their system went down, everything went with it."

"But you'd think written reference would be made to something so disastrous—even years later?" said Lee.

"Maybe it didn't seem *disastrous* until it was too late?" suggested Tai. "And then it became pointless?"

Gareth sat listening, trying to keep awake. The big room was warm and too bright, with lights they had brought in from their tents. Like herself and Paul, who sat next to the fireplace wrapped in a blanket, they all showed the effects of illness. Lee Hamlin's cheeks and eyes were hollow; Major Singh wheezed. Tai and Wesley Hall looked tired after nearly a week of nursing the whole compound. And Paul . . . she tried not to see how frail and thin he was.

Paul had come over out of kindness, to spare her the burden of being alone with the visitors. Margo had refused with the excuse of being tired. "Which is the truth," she told Gareth. "I never saw people ask so many questions. You answer one and they think of five more. I haven't talked so much before in my whole life. It's very wearing. I'm beginning to wonder if people didn't drive the Builders out just to get some peace and quiet."

It was raining, a cold, steady rain that began in late afternoon and lingered and, they said, deafened them with its drumming on their tents. They had been apologetic, almost bashful when they asked if they could come inside for the evening. It surprised Gareth that these people who seemed so supremely capable could be made to look so lonely in the rain, and she had felt herself ungracious for not thinking of inviting them indoors; they deserved more of her regard than that. How strange it must be for them to feel so far from home on a rainy night.

One of the village boys who'd come to visit her that day had said the strangers reminded him of hive insects when they arrived in a sudden silvery swarm. They ran about, making noises, stinging and subduing and lugging people off to their nest. "And then," he said, "you told us they were *people* and meant no harm at all, that they'd come to help us—but in such a way that everybody nearly died of fright." He said he had to laugh at people "who were so smart they were stupid."

That was apparently how most of the villagers felt now that they were over being scared—that the visitors were a source of wonder and amusement, as well as medical care. The ulcers had stopped hurting; several people who had been crazy for years were rational again; they cured pneumonia. Before they went away again, Gareth wanted them to teach her all they could. But they seemed more interested in asking questions than sharing knowledge.

"Gareth?" Paul's tone suggested he had called her name before. "Are you sleeping with your eyes open?"

"Maybe," she admitted. "I'm sorry. What did you ask me?"

"The top book on the pile I left there on the table—would you see if you can read any of it into the translator?" he asked, and then explained to the others, "It's the oldest in our house, and the writing is so poor we've never been able to make sense of it."

Gareth reached across and got the book. Its leather cover was so dry with age that she could feel it powdering in her grasp.

Another book that should be copied before it turned to dust—when there was time. She opened it; there was no title, author's name, or date inside. Separating the fragile pages, she studied the first paragraph, and then began:

"I never knew a man could lose all hope. It is a slow and enervating process, this dehydration of the soul."

The translator paused. In the quiet a log in the fireplace burned through and fell. Orange sparks showered down onto the hearth.

"They won't return to Xilan. We've had no message from them in more than ten years Xilan time. No other ship has called. I go out at night and watch for them."

An insect buzzed the lamp. Gareth batted it away with a practiced offhand gesture that whacked the bug onto the floor where a pet walla waited to crunch it like a piece of fallen popcorn. She glanced up at her audience before continuing to read. They were watching her, waiting.

"The people who brought us here must be old by now. How many years passed on Earth before the ships returned? When they got back, were they celebrated as the colonizers of Xilan? Or were they boring history, something curious from the past, worthy only of a final thirty-second item on the evening news? Who cares about a single planet, light years from Earth and all that matters. How old am I in real years?"

"It confirms what you told us, but not all of it makes sense to me." Gareth broke the silence that followed the translation. "And it's very sad." She looked to the four for an explanation, but none seemed to want to talk.

"Please go on," Lee urged.

Not sure she wanted to know more of this, Gareth sighed but continued reading.

"Corporations are only groups of people. I see that now. One has time to see clearly here. People sold us the land; people brought ten thousand of us here. Profits made on our hope and ignorance provided ease for their old age. I wonder, do they ever think of us, those faceless people who sold land on worlds they've never seen? Who designed the very attractive real estate brochure? Do they know how hard we have to work?"

He sounds as unreal as these people, Gareth thought as she listened to the words. Without knowing why, she felt impatient with the person who had written this journal—she pictured him standing outside in the dark, staring up at the stars and feeling sorry for himself. She didn't know why he should; Xilan was a beautiful world.

She read on, several pages of questions, all vilifying people who had brought and left the writer there. "Where did you find this book?" she asked Paul when the translator had finished with the passage.

"In a storeroom," he said. "It's very old."

"It's very tiresome," she said and closed it.

"May I read it?" Lee asked, and Gareth gave it to her.

"He probably wasn't far from the truth—the man who wrote that," said Major Singh. "I think they were forgotten. It's logical that back then by the time the ships returned to Earth two or three generations had passed. Priorities change. Records get lost. Unless someone specifically orders research . . ." He shrugged. "Things get overlooked, lost in the cracks. It was nothing underhanded—it just was that way."

Gareth didn't understand that, even with the translator. She opened another ancient instruction book of some kind, full of drawings of symbols and patterned structures and strange mathematical formulas. She couldn't read more than a word or sentence here and there.

"How old is that?" Lee asked, catching sight of an illustration as Gareth turned the pages. "When did they start manually storing such technical data?"

"You mean how long did it take for the computer system to go out—or be in danger?" asked Wes. "Good point. It evidently didn't happen overnight." He got up and came over to the table to look over Gareth's shoulder. "Could you go back to the very front, please?" and when she did, he read the words on the cover page: "Basic Principles of Organic Chemistry, Klaus and Birk-hauer, Academic Data Ltd., Toronto, transcribed by Norman Bloch, Xilan year 28."

"So soon?"

"Looks like it."

"That's the oldest one I've seen."

As the four talked among themselves, Gareth checked the other books Paul had brought up from storage. All looked technical, like the one Wes was glancing through, and to her a waste of time so far as telling them anything about real people. She slipped out of her chair and went into the next room where her parents had kept especially precious volumes. In the light from the open door she searched the shelves of an old cupboard, until her fingers touched the crumbling leather of the five oldest personal journals in the compound. She had always meant to read them but had never had the time. Now she eased all five out of their space on the shelf, intending to take them in, then hesitated. If the visitors saw them, knew they existed, they might ask to copy them, as Lee had asked to copy many of the books she'd read. The personal lives of Mitchell ancestors were really none of their business. She rose, brushed off her hands, and went back into the light.

They refused her invitation to sleep in the house. She didn't know why; there were more than enough beds. Puzzled, she walked her guests to the door and watched them run to their tents, silver rain streaking past their lamps. Their tents glowed to life as they gained shelter. Rain gusted against the doorstep and water in the spouting gargled as it drained into the cistern. It was what her father had called "a night not fit for man nor beast." She closed the door and walked back down the hall.

"Who's been feeding the barn animals and chasing the chickens in to roost while we've been sick?" she asked Paul as she settled onto the lounge next to him.

"Tai and Wesley Hall," he said. "They took care of the animals. The chickens enjoyed total freedom." He flipped the corner of his blanket over her bare feet. "Why didn't you bring out the old journals? Those may be the ones they need, you know."

Gareth looked from his face into the fire. "Maybe," she agreed. "How did you know I was going to?"

He smiled and shook his head as if she'd asked a silly question. "I know you, and this house, and where your footsteps led. What made you change your mind?"

"I decided those books were none of their business."

"They mean well, for all their strangeness," he said gently. "They saved our lives."

"They made us sick."

"And we returned the favor," he reminded her. "They seem to be basically good people. I know their approach is sometimes condescending—as if we existed only for them to arrive and study us. But one must try to see things from the other's point of view." He stared into the fire and then shook his head. "I can't imagine what their lives are like—living in their ship, being shut in almost constantly, never seeing sun or rain or moonlight. They're prisoners, really. Wesley Hall told me how he looks forward to coming to a world. He said Xilan reminds him of Earth, his world. We had long talks together."

"Did he tell you what they plan to do once they know everything about us?" Gareth asked.

"He doesn't know. Nothing, I imagine. Go away again."

"They're saying, or that journal said, we're a five-hundred-year-old mistake. That the Builders brought people here and abandoned them."

"Yes," Paul agreed. "I got that impression, too."

"Doesn't it bother you?"

"Why? It may be true. And if it is, we may be the lucky ones. I wouldn't like their kind of life."

"They're going to the cube tomorrow if it doesn't rain. Singh says there's a way to get inside."

"They'd enter it?" he asked, surprised.

"If they can. They asked me to go with them."

Paul considered that idea. "They know of the sounds it makes?" and when she nodded, "Are you going? Is that wise?"

"There's no monster in there, Paul," she said, and smiled at his look of concern.

"Not of flesh and blood," he agreed. "But sometimes it's a mistake to know too much."

CHAPTER
19

ONE LOOK AT THE HILL ON WHICH THE CUBE STOOD AND Gareth felt as if someone she loved had just been killed. The ground looked as if a giant creature had been burrowing and gone berserk. Mounds of raw red dirt were heaped beside deep trenches, which exposed walls beneath the cube. Trees had been pushed over and torn out by the roots. Other trees were slashed and barked so that they too would die. The path along the cliff was gone, strewn with debris. Overburden spilled onto the beach below. Red mud stained the waves.

Instead of rising majestically above the trees, the cube stood exposed, reduced to a brutal block of rusting metal, an eyesore, visible for miles.

"What have you done?" she whispered, shocked, unable to accept what she saw. "What have you done?"

Her voice was so low only Major Singh heard her question.

"I had my construction crew fly up and dig out access to the labs under the telescope," he said, and added proudly, "Didn't take them long either. Once they compared our pictures with the satellite shots, they knew just where to dig. The weight of the structure sits on bedrock—"

"You had no right! You've ruined it! Destroyed it!"

"It's not ruined. You'll see." He was intent on landing and paying no real attention to her. "The structure's still intact. That northwest hillside had been flowing down over it all these years. They should have put a retainer wall up there. Soil moves with rain—"

"It will take a hundred years for time to hide this scar," she said, mourning. "Trees grow so slowly . . . most had escaped the fire."

"You've got a whole world full of trees." Safely landed now, he glanced over the seat at her, his face puzzled, as if he were trying to imagine what he'd done that displeased her, and she realized he truly did not know.

"Why can't you understand?" she asked. "It was all one. It belonged! The villagers in total madness couldn't have done a tenth of this—made it ugly, for all my lifetime and my children's. It was ours. . . ."

"But you didn't even know what it was," he said. "How could it matter?"

The hatch dropped down; the sweet smells of plowed ground and crushed wood poured in. Her eyes welled with tears. Before the other four could move, she was out and running across the rubble, scattering flocks of birds and lizards hunting grubs in the loose soil. As she ran she passed some village men walking beside the trench. They were looking down at walls no one here had guessed existed.

"They did a good job," one of the men called. "They exposed the roots and killed it. The thing hasn't turned since."

She looked from his face to the ruin looming up against the morning sky, to the spot where a grove of ancient silkwoods had stood yesterday—and for three hundred years before. Now pieces of their roots lay mangled at the bottom of a trench, crushed in muddy machine tracks. She thought of all the times she'd come up here to sit beneath those trees, the grace of them, the whisper of their leaves. It was all gone, destroyed without a thought, along with all the joy she'd felt here, along with the peace and the past. And she felt a grief almost as deep as that when her parents died. This place had been her friend, and she had loved it dearly.

"A good job." The words echoed in her mind. That was what they thought too—"Didn't take them long." A hard knot formed in her chest and traveled up to her throat in a strangled sob. She turned and ran, tear-blinded, down the ruined path along the sea, toward home.

"Gareth?" Lee called, and then she caught a glimpse of the girl's face and felt her own eyes blur. Something in that stricken look shot home, and she knew they were guilty of inflicting an unforgivable pain.

"Where's she going?" called Major Singh.

"Away from us," Lee said.

"Why? Doesn't she want to see what it is?"

"It's apparently what it was that mattered."

"But she didn't know. . . . We had to dig it up."

"No," Lee agreed. "She didn't know. Now she does."

"I don't understand," the major said. "We told her we were going inside. She didn't seem upset." He stood watching Gareth run until she was a tiny figure far down the beach, and then he shook his head. "I thought she'd be interested. . . . Let's go."

Lee hesitated, trying to understand what had caused the degree of grief she'd seen on the girl's face. It was almost like her own when she had seen . . .

"You coming?"

"Yes."

"Stop thinking. It doesn't pay to think."

They followed him to an oblong opening in one wall of a trench and stepped through it into darkness. The vestibule was thick with the remains of roots and mud, but the tunnel-like inner hall was empty and secure.

In the light Wesley Hall carried, the place looked like a distorted version of the storerooms under Gareth's house. In some rooms white roots of trees had thrust up through the floor and writhed around to anchor themselves on furniture. The roots looked strangely alive, as if they stopped moving when the light struck them. Most rooms, including the data storage center, were intact, their walls lined with screens and dials, their centers occupied by chairs and tables. Dust coated everything so thickly it appeared to be sprayed on.

Lee filmed it all, particularly a room where streaks of moving light were visible beneath the dusty screens, and tiny needles moved in dials.

The hallway angled right, sloped downward, and they were walking in surface water that seeped through the walls. "We're under the rim of the MMT now," Singh told them as they splashed along.

The water ended as the hall sloped upward toward a sliding door, half open, clogged by drifted sand and dust shaped by centuries of drafts into a high dune. Dust-thick light from the room beyond streamed through the door.

They entered and were at the base of a ramp near one side of a single enormous room. The walls were eighty feet high; the ceiling distant and girdered. Two-thirds of the space was occupied by the telescope itself, a mass of dull metal—long barrels, pipes, bars, and beams—tilted at an angle toward the "eye," but from here, inside, the eye was only isolated triangles of opaque glass. The floor was crowded with antique computer equipment, and catwalks led to various levels where there was still more.

"Xilan supply, this is Inventory Control." The voice boomed from an amplifier far above their heads, and everybody jumped. "Cencon reports you low on carbohydrates. Please check and confirm?"

"That you, Nancy?"

"Yes. Marshall?"

"Right!"

"How are things down there?"

"Boring, but somebody's gotta get stuck with surface duty."

"Better you than me. You want to check your bulk container carbohydrates?"

"Hang on."

The booming voices stopped. For a moment the four just

looked at one another. "That's their ghostly voices from the cube," the major realized. "Space chatter. It's picking up radio transmissions between ship and base. There's an open receiver in here. They put it on the amplifiers—I don't know why—"

"Think," Lee said. "That man's diary, remember? He said they hadn't *heard* a ship in ten years? Maybe this was the last receiver that worked—and they put it on amplification so they could hear a call even when no one was in here. . . ."

"And by the time another ship—our ship—reached this star system, the people here had forgotten what it was." Wesley Hall finished the thought, and they stood silent for a time, thinking of those who waited long ago for a rescue ship that never came.

"But why does this building still operate?" wondered Major Singh. "Those cells around the mirrors aren't big enough to power this place."

"Its skin," said Tai. "Its outer shell—"

"We have fourteen cases of Type A in stock, three cases of C-Pro," the loudspeaker blared. They were forced to listen to the subsequent ordering of supplies and small talk between the crewmen before they could continue their own conversation.

"Do you think we could turn that off?" Wesley Hall asked.

"Probably," said the major, "but I don't want to touch anything. This place is an artifact. As Margo said—move something and it may never work again. This equipment is so old that I can only guess how it works. Besides, let the astrophysicists mess it up. It's their responsibility. What were you saying about the outer shell, Tai?"

"It absorbs solar radiation. There's a thermo-regulatory system built into the shell, and energy is stored beneath us somewhere. I can feel the flow."

"You mean it's an older version of our ship's hull?" Major Singh asked, frowning. "Would that generate enough power to move this bulk against surface gravity?"

"Maybe. It rotates on a friction-free mount; the turntable should move almost forever."

"Let's let the experts speculate," suggested Lee. "All we have to do is tell them what's working—if we can. Let's finish and get out of here."

The four of them left the compound that afternoon. They took with them, "for analyses," all the books they'd borrowed—which they promised to return. They left behind three circles of dead grass where their tents had stood, a blackened area they had lasered to dispose of insects feeding on the plants, and one sanit module concealed among the ruins.

For the next few days there was a lot of activity up at the cube. Air trucks came and went. Silver-suited people hurried in and out, carrying things. Gareth didn't go to watch as most of the villagers did. She tried not to think about it and felt foolish at remembering her old surety that joy had happened there. Instead she busied herself trying to re-establish her normal life: cleaning the kitchen, gardening, preparing and putting away the medicinals she'd gathered on her trip. She visited those people still recovering from the flu, listened to their experiences with the strangers, and tried not to think about what was happening and would happen to their world.

C H A P T E R
20

"THEY'LL UNDERSTAND US BETTER IF THEY SEE HOW WE LIVE," Lee said. "And perhaps forgive us."

"I've strict orders against allowing them in camp." Commander Nathan did not look at her as he spoke but closely examined his pen. "The executive staff wants the colonists isolated, kept as pure as possible until the social scientists have all the data they need."

"But how would letting just Paul and Gareth visit upset anything?"

His eyes met hers again. "They're influential members of the group, aren't they?"

Lee hesitated. "I don't know. They seem to be respected—"

"And therefore influential. We can't afford to inflict too much culture shock on them—have them carry back distorted reports of what we're like." He rose to end the interview. "Be patient, Dr. Hamlin. You've made friends with them. Your outlook is no longer objective."

"Have you learned anything from the old MMT?" she asked as she got up to leave. "The grapevine says the astrophysicists salvaged an immense amount of data."

"And all of it incidental to this expedition," said Nathan, then to soften his brusqueness added, "I'm told there may be evidence of solar flare-ups intense enough to expand Xilan's atmosphere to the point where it enveloped all orbiting satellites. If that happened, the atmospheric gases would have created drag on the energy collectors, slowed them into decaying orbits and eventual crash."

"And there went the colony's power source?"

"Most of it. Exactly." His tone congratulated her on her perception.

It wasn't until later, walking back to the lab, that Lee realized he hadn't really said anything concrete, not regarding Paul and Gareth's visit or anything else. Anyone could speculate on sun storms. It made a valid excuse for the colony's failure—an act of God beyond corporate control or individual responsibility. But every lab test she ran hinted it was man and not God who had originally erred here.

Confined to base to help analyze and process the multitude of specimens collected in the colony, she was beginning to wonder on what basis had this planet been judged safe for colonial settlement. Was knowledge so limited or tests so crude five hundred years before that problems hadn't been foreseen? She was finding chemical and mineral compounds so strange that no chemist would have ever thought them possible, and finding them in villagers' blood and tissue samples, as well as in some of the fruits and vegetables they ate. Their hams contained almost lethal amounts of sea salt rich in metals. The computer said humans could not tolerate such food, and yet these people did.

She no longer wondered at the old diary's remark, "Children die so easily—just slip away." She found it extraordinary that any had survived. Surely her colleagues had similar questions? Yet no one voiced them aloud—or if they did, not to her. Like the commander, everyone seemed to be avoiding saying anything, herself included.

Ever since they'd discovered the colonists, the atmosphere of the expedition had changed, become muddled and disorganized. No one was doing his regular job. All routine assignments and the habits that went with routine had been displaced. Everything focused on the colonials, and everything about those people was disturbing. But no one wanted to commit himself, to say what he thought out loud. If corporate fraud had been involved in settling the original colony . . . but then real estate fraud was as old as the history of man.

The piercing cry of a red kite made Lee glance up to see one bank in a graceful glide above the beach. The cry was answered by another kite which joined the first, and the pair played on the wind. She hadn't seen kites at the base before and wondered if they were partial to human inhabitation. Some alien creatures were, enjoying the noise and activity. Or just curious. The view of the surf and offshore islands reminded her of the jade-green seals she'd seen the first morning here. That morning seemed a long time past.

"It's a beautiful world, isn't it?" Wesley Hall's voice made her jump. She'd been so preoccupied she hadn't seen him approach. "It's hard to believe it may be unfit for human consumption." He was watching the red kites, not looking at her.

"You're getting that impression, too?"

He nodded. "I'm doing an indepth study of urine samples—a poor way to get to know one's fellowman, but revealing."

"And?"

"It's not only hard work that makes them die by the age of forty. That any live that long is a tribute to the human kidney. And I would bet, if we could trace their medical history back through the generations, that only the healthiest stock survived this long."

"Have you seen any complete physicals?" she asked.

"Some were done in the village, especially on those with acute copper poisoning, but the computer tells me the data is either incomplete or invalid."

A utility cart rolled by, its fat doughnut tires plowing silky furrows in the sand, its freight bed stacked high with clean linens for the staff quarters. The driver waved as she passed.

"The commander says solar flare-ups may have destroyed their energy satellites and blacked them out," Lee said.

"And if that hadn't happened, the colony would have prospered?" Wesley Hall asked.

"He didn't say that."

"And I won't believe it if he does. What have you been working on?"

She told him. He nodded at intervals but did not interrupt. "What do you think?" she asked him when she'd finished. "The ignorance of the time? Or carelessness combined with greed on the part of colonial real estate speculators?"

He shrugged. "All the above? Until we get definite information we can only guess. They may have begun to die off so quickly that before twenty years passed there were too few left to care for each other properly."

"But die of what?"

"Malnutrition. Slow starvation. Or, if there were flare-ups, solar radiation."

"Then how did any survive?"

"I don't know." He spoke so softly she could barely hear him. "I don't know. There are thousands of possibilities. Is it diet, gravity, or atmosphere that enlarges their hearts? They have amino acids we've never seen before. We're supposed to learn how this all happened, Lee, and I don't think we can. I look at all the work—"

"Stop it!" She had never seen Wesley Hall depressed, and this uncharacteristic despair disturbed her. "Stop it! It's not your fault. You're the one who always tells me to stop thinking. Take your own advice. That colony is not your responsibility."

"Not on Xilan, no." He turned and looked at her, and it seemed to Lee that he had aged without her noticing the change until now. There were lines deep in his face, and his eyes were soul-weary. "Not on Xilan. But, Lee, suppose that our dreams of colonizing space are based on hope and ignorance? Suppose we can visit any world we like, but we cannot live there? Suppose we are creatures of Earth, uniquely designed by four billion years of the ever-increasing molecular complexity called evolution to fit

Earth's environment and only Earth's? Suppose we can create artificial worlds that match the conditions of our home, but there is no other natural world to which we can adapt and on which we can survive and endure? Suppose all that is true?"

"But we've colonized fourteen planets, Wes. And they're prospering."

"Have you been to any of the new worlds since they were settled?"

"No . . . but thousands of people go each year. New settlers —they wouldn't go if it wasn't safe."

"So we're told . . . but still I'd like to see some proof now. Something to reassure myself that we haven't been participating in the creation of other Xilans."

She stared at him, not wanting to consider the enormity of what he was suggesting. It just couldn't be true. "The data we collect is all correlated, Wes. We don't make mistakes like that."

"Are you sure?" He walked away to leave her wondering if he was right—would any alien world support human life on a long-term basis? After many expensive but disastrous attempts there had been no more extraterrestrial zoos on Earth; the animals always died or stopped breeding despite the finest care. None of the planetary colonies was as old as this one—and she had never visited any after settlement. Suppose a missing enzyme or a mold or bacteria was all it took to cause long-term disaster?

She watched Wes cross the green, en route to the lab dome. He didn't look back or wave, and she thought again as she often did how much easier it was to work with animals than people. Animals might wound or chew one up, but they never caused harrowing introspection or self-doubt.

There was an easy way to check it out. All it took was time and access to the emigration and census statistics for planetary colonies. She could see no point in brooding over questions when

answers were as close as the ship's reference library. Why hadn't
he thought of that? She hurried back to her lab cubicle, sure she
could solve the problem.

An hour later she wasn't so sure. Not because of what she'd
learned but because of what she hadn't. All the data she
requested was listed: "Classified, Type A-1 Clearance Only." She
tried another tack. "Tell me," she asked the Reference Library's
voice, "which Xilan surface personnel have A-1 clearance?"

"Group Commander Nathan and Lieutenant Daniels."

"Thank you." Lee left the lab so quickly she missed the
automatic, "You're welcome."

Lieutenant Daniels wasn't in his office, and since his was the
only chair, she sat there to wait for him. Empty minutes passed.
She stared at the papers on the desk.

"Confidential" said a large red stamp across the face of a top
sheet, and in smaller, redder print, "Preliminary—Not for
Distribution". Directly beneath this inviting notice was a distribution list, against which Commander Nathan's name was
checked. The printout format was that of a report in memo form
for easy editing. To pass the time, she leaned forward and began
to read:

PRELIMINARY REPORT TO THE EXECUTIVE COMMITTEE
RE: COLONIAL FEASIBILITY STUDY, PLANET XILAN, TUR-
FAN SYSTEM, PLANETARY TITLE NUMBER: 27032951,
ISSUED BY 2507 TO: VERDE-HENDRICK LTD., A SUBSIDI-
ARY OF LVL DEVELOPMENT CORP., NEW PERTH REGIS-
TRY. REPORT PREPARED BY: W. A. SAMOF, BS, MS, PHD;
C. Y. T. CHANG, PHD; AND T. HOBART DESMOND, PHD;
NPC DEPARTMENT OF SOCIAL SCIENCES, WITH SUPPLE-
MENTAL INPUT BY L. SHOUP, MBS, PHD, NPC, DEPART-
MENT OF ECONOMICS.

Her eyes tended to glaze when she read this sort of thing. The
self-importance implied by the careful inclusion of all the writers'

initials and degrees always struck her as a perverted form of
scenting, a spraying of academic musk to mark dominance in a
specific territory.

> SUMMARY: WHILE THE PROTOTYPE TEST COLONY
> FAILED, NO LIABILITY CAN BE AFFIXED TO THE CORPO-
> RATION, NOR DOES THE ORIGINAL COLONY'S FAILURE
> PRECLUDE DEVELOPMENT POTENTIAL.

She scanned the pages. It was called a feasibility study,
implying a future project, yet this paper concerned itself solely
with the authors' observations of the present colony, observations
so clinical in tone that they could have concerned a colony of rats.

> THE SUBJECTS FAILED TO MAINTAIN THEIR ORIGINAL
> HABITAT AND SOCIAL STRUCTURE. THEY SHOW POOR
> COLONIZING ABILITIES. THEIR BEHAVIOR PATTERNS
> CAN BE TERMED ABERRANT. SURVIVORS EXHIBIT
> MARKED PHYSICAL AND SOCIOLOGICAL VARIATIONS
> FROM THE ROOT STOCK. SOME PHYSIOLOGICAL PHE-
> NOMENA MAY BE ATTRIBUTABLE TO ENVIRONMENTAL
> FACTORS.

She scanned several pages of physical "abnormalities" and
came to:

> BREEDING STRATEGY OBVIOUSLY FAILED. SURPLUS OFF-
> SPRING WERE UNAVAILABLE TO EMIGRATE: NO NEW
> COLONIES WERE ESTABLISHED. THE BASE POPULATION
> DETERIORATED, POPULATION MONITORING PROCE-
> DURES WERE IGNORED. INBREEDING IN ISOLATION RE-
> DUCED GENETIC DIVERSITY.
> ADULTS OF EACH SEX PRESENTLY OCCUPY A STABLE
> HOME RANGE WITH AN OCCASIONAL OVERLAP OF ADULT
> FEMALES AND JUVENILES. BREEDING ADULTS DIE OFF
> WITH LIMITED REPLACEMENT.
> IT IS THE WRITERS' JOINT OPINION THAT, SHOULD WE

DECIDE TO RECOLONIZE XILAN, THE PRESENT POPULA-
TION BE REMOVED. SUCH ACTION, WHILE COSTLY,
WOULD AVOID UNNECESSARY NEGATIVE RESPONSE
FROM NEW EMIGRANTS IN THE ALL-IMPORTANT
FIRST-IMPRESSION PHASE OF RESETTLEMENT.
RECOMMENDATIONS: (1) EVACUATE REMAINING POPULA-
TION TO TEMPORARY REFUGEE QUARTERS NEAR NEW
PERTH AND RETAIN THEM THERE FOR FURTHER STUDY
WHILE PERMANENT HOUSING IS PREPARED (NOTE: IT IS
THE JOINT OPINION OF THE AUTHORS THAT, DUE TO
THE OVERALL CONDITION OF THESE SUBJECTS, REHA-
BILITATION MAY PROVE IMPOSSIBLE. THEY AND THEIR
OFFSPRING MAY REMAIN WARDS OF THE STATE.)

An asterisk indicated a footnote which referred to a report in
progress covering the estimated cost of the evacuation and
projected cost of the refugees' maintenance.

(2) AFTER EVACUATION OF THE PRESENT POPULATION,
ALL TRACES OF THE HABITATION SHOULD BE EXCISED
AND THE SITE REFORESTED OR OTHERWISE COSMETI-
CALLY TREATED.
(3) ANY FUTURE SITES SHOULD BE WELL REMOVED
FROM THIS AREA.

Her hands were shaking as she lay the papers back onto the
pile, then carefully realigned them, as if neatness counted in the
face of monstrousness. She stood staring at the square of sunlight
on the floor, her thoughts battering themselves against the
ethical cage of her mind. There was no escape; she knew that
immediately; no way to disassociate herself from this. On impulse she picked up the report again and put it through the
copier at the side of the desk.

She was walking out the door when Lieutenant Daniels
entered. "Did you want something, Dr. Hamlin?" he asked her
as she passed. She neither saw nor heard him.

What she saw was Gareth and her people being rounded up
and herded onto shuttles, enclosed for a year or more aboard the
Kekule in cargo holds, the only quarters large enough for them,
saw them transformed from self-sufficiency into wards of the
state, or patients—most probably patients. For if they were like
most creatures removed from their habitat, trauma alone would
cause most to fall ill or die. And if new colonists came here, what
proof was there that they wouldn't end up like Gareth's people?
Did all colonies end like that? She turned on her heel and went
back to Daniels' office.

"Why can't I get statistics on the planet-based colonies?"

He stared up at her for a moment, startled from his work, then
asked, "That's A-1 clearance data?"

"So I'm told."

He nodded, tapped several keys of his computer and waited for
the screen to answer. "Access is restricted to the ship's executive
staff and the sociology group."

"Why?"

"I have no idea, Dr. Hamlin," he said pleasantly enough.
"That's not my job."

Dead end—unless she asked Commander Nathan, and at the
present time she suspected he too would avoid answering her by
a more sophisticated variation on the theme of "It's not my job."
Lieutenant Daniels' eyes were so innocently blue. Sunlight
touched his hair and red-gold glinted. He kept his compact body
trim, immaculate, in his blue uniform. So clean, so decent-
looking a specimen. So sure of his responsibilities. Why did she
feel the urge to scream?

"Was there anything else, Dr. Hamlin?"

"No. Not that you could help me with. Thank you."

She went back to the lab and made a copy of the report for
everyone in camp. Wesley Hall helped her distribute them.
Before another hour passed the commander called her to his
office.

"Why?" he asked as she walked in. He held a copy of the report.

"I can't condone it."

"You weren't asked to. It was confidential. You know better—"

"So do you, Commander. How could you accept that with no comment—"

"Basic research people never understand management's long-term objectives."

"But I'm beginning to," said Lee. "Like any organism, the corporation is programmed to survive and reproduce. It does anything it has to in order to perpetuate itself." She smiled as another idea occurred to her. "That understanding gives all new meaning to the term *company man*."

"Is that all you think I am?"

"No. I respected you. . . ."

"Past tense," he noted sadly. His eyes became more hooded, more impersonal, and he shifted in his chair, away from her. "We have no definite proof this world is unsafe. Granted it may be less than ideal. Few planets are ideal. But people have to go somewhere, have to immigrate—if not to this, then to some other world that might be worse. And people have survived here—with no support. There has to be a trade-off between idealism and what must be done, Dr. Hamlin. We have to consider the greatest good for the greatest number."

"Do you truly believe that's what's involved here?"

"I must," he said simply. "Without that faith I'm lost. So are we all."

For a moment Lee felt the same intense anxiety she knew each time the shuttle left the ship, the feeling of being trapped in a situation far beyond her control, diminished and disoriented. Incidental.

"I talked to Stevens about the uproar this report is causing," Nathan was saying. "He's VP in Charge of Planning. He's very upset that it was leaked in preliminary form. I reminded him that if he went ahead with these recommendations there was no way he could keep it secret. He feels the colonists here might be grateful for the chance to come with us."

"Has he asked them?"

"He's basing his opinion on the reports of his people. From what I've seen, I tend to agree with him. Why would any intelligent being remain in a hardship survival situation if they had a choice?"

"Excuse me, sir," Lieutenant Daniels interrupted on the intercom, "but I thought you'd want to know. The field crew assigned to research the village is flying back to camp."

"Why? Were they attacked?"

"No, sir. They've apparently decided to strike over the contents of that report." There was a slight pause, and then the lieutenant added. "I *am* sorry, sir," and in that apology Lee heard the young man's plea to be somehow forgiven for letting the troublesome document be exposed on his desk. The intercom clicked off.

Seconds passed in silence while the commander stared at a point somewhere above her head. She stood waiting.

"Apparently many of the research staff lack my faith," he said finally.

CHAPTER 21

More than a week has passed, and our visitors have not returned, Gareth wrote in her journal. *I didn't like this last group. They treated us with less respect than Uri treats his pigs. The villagers are hoping they won't come back so they can keep the tent for storing cordwood. They're afraid to touch the equipment left behind and have told Paul he's welcome to it for parts—but they get first choice of all wheels.*

Paul is much improved, and Margo's well again. I've done what Tai suggested and fed them only chicken and vegetables—no ham—and while both he and Margo complain about their diet, both are looking better. The chickens are starting to avoid me. I'll have to go fishing soon or severely deplete my flock. I don't like fish. The village bakery reopened today, and the mill is running again.

Haying begins tomorrow. Everyone who can will be working in the fields. It's a good time of year. The fields smell sweet—

Her pen stopped as she stared off into the memory of a summer evening with a pale green sky and perfect stars; she was riding atop a load of hay with the other children, her parents walking ahead with the team. All her world was safe and known then. The Builders were only a bedtime story . . .

The building creaked, as it settled deeper into sleep, and woke her from a doze. She yawned and closed her journal. Before blowing out the lamp, she took a feather from the pen box and removed two insects from the oil, flicking them into the fireplace.

"Out, Herman."

The walla sleeping under her desk grudgingly roused itself and followed her to the door.

It was her habit, and had been her mother's, to check the weather before going to bed each night. The air smelled of lemonberry blossoms; she made a mental note to gather some to replace those in the drawers. The night was still and clear, the star canopy bright. That meant high cold winds and low humidity, good for haying.

She had just glimpsed a falling star high in the western sky when Herman, having felt the temperature, tried to sneak back into the house. "No, you don't!" she said, and stuck out a leg to stop him. "You go sleep in the barn." As she shoved him gently backward on the path, he dug his toes in and raked gravel until she reached back and shut the door behind them. He quit resisting then and sat staring sadly up at her, his eyes shining in the dim light from Margo's dome. "Begging won't help," she told him.

When she looked back up at that section of the sky where the falling star had been, she was surprised to see it still there, still falling, winking brightly as it passed overhead and took several minutes to reach the eastern horizon. She'd never seen such a deliberate star before. Meteors arced and disappeared, or were seen only as a trace of light as they burned in the atmosphere. And then it dawned on her that this star was high above the atmosphere, like a new moon orbiting the world, and she understood that what she'd seen was the Builders' ship. It was real, not a story.

Until now she'd half believed they'd lied, that they lived somewhere on Xilan. Until now she hadn't truly understood the gulf between herself and these strangers, the difference between

where she stood and that starlike object that had passed overhead. They were so far above; their knowledge was so great.

She leaned back against the wooden door, terrified. Had her
people known all that once? Had they lost so much?

They had cut halfway across the first hayfield when the
airtrucks returned. Gareth had just congratulated herself on the
artistry of her scythe swath that fanned the falling stalks evenly
for drying; they looked as skilled as any farmer's. The field was
full of wallas alert for the insects and small animals fleeing before
the mowers and rakers. People called to one another, joking as
they worked, glad to be up and about again, doing something
familiar. They wore wide-brimmed straw hats against the sun,
and many of the men were shirtless. Children wandered the
windrows, carrying water jugs or running with the wallas.

They heard the airtrucks' high-pitched whine before they saw
them. The whole field went still. Gareth felt her stomach knot
with nerves. What did they want now? Were they coming back to
return the things they'd taken "for analyses," or perhaps to get
their tent? She leaned on the scythe and waited. The yellow
aircraft came into view above the sea, to the left of the devastated
cliff. There were three of them. They landed beside the tent.

From the hillside field, they could see the crews emerge, shiny
dots in the distance that seemed to float like dust motes against
the green background. Several drifted down the village street
and disappeared behind the houses. Others went into the tent.

"They've probably come to take it down," she heard Luther
say. "I never thought they'd leave something that big behind."
He sounded disappointed all the same.

"You think we should go see what they want?" another man
asked.

"Why waste the time?" said Ula, Luther's wife. "They'll do
what they want regardless. If we don't like it they'll knock us out
like they did before—'for our own good'—and do it anyhow.
Let's get on with haying."

"But they haven't harmed us," Luther said. "They're people the same as we are."

"So they say." The woman spoke as if to a child too young to disillusion. Several people laughed. With her free hand she swept off her hat and wiped her forehead against her arm, replaced the hat and went back to raking.

"They made the cube quit talking," Luther said.

"Not for our sakes," she answered and went on raking grass into a row.

"You always look on the dark side," Luther said, and began to remind her of the details of his illness and rapid recovery.

Gareth lifted her scythe and went back to work. Luther was talking more loudly than he needed to—for her benefit. Her skills had lost standing in the eyes of some villagers. They knew she couldn't do half the things the strangers' medical machine could do. They ascribed magical powers to the medical machines. Between that and the fact that the cube was associated with her family, she knew her position in the community had subtly changed, and not for the better. Not that anyone was rude; they still needed her, but that knowledge galled.

"They're carrying out the equipment," a sharp-eyed boy reported. "I can see them loading it into the fliers."

That information seemed to relax the tension in the field. Within minutes the uneven rows of mowers were at work again. But the sense of ease and peace was gone, along with the laughing banter. Those who talked discussed the strangers. The scythes made rhythmic swishing noises as they flashed through the tall grass. The rakes clattered and rustled. Wallas hopped and barked and hunted, undisturbed by the arrival of new aliens, as intent upon the moment as they had been for fifty million years.

An hour passed before a new noise interrupted the work—the sound of loudspeakers in the village.

An airtruck lifted off and came down the valley. Its approach drowned out the distant noises. By the time it was overhead, it was flying so low that Gareth could see people inside. They wore helmets and silver suits, and she wondered if they were still afraid of germs. Jet wash thrashed the grass still standing and rolled windrows into tangled piles.

"Attention!" The word boomed down at them. Wallas exploded into arcing hops of panic. Children shrieked and ran. "Don't be afraid." The words were slow and distinct. "Come back to the village. We will show you pictures of our world. Put down your tools and come. The pictures will be shown in the tent."

The workers stared up against the wind that whipped hair into their eyes and made sleeves billow. Rows of hay began to lift and fall as if they were breathing and then blow and scatter.

"Get higher! You're ruining the field!" Gareth shouted. Her words were blown away. She waved them off, mimed a lifting motion, pointed at the blowing windrows. "Go away!" Others joined in shouting, and some waved the nuisance off with their rakes and scythes and long-handled sickles.

The airtruck circled slowly, those inside staring at the spectacle below, then lifted and moved off to circle the almost empty compound and shout instructions to it before returning to the village.

"Pictures?" a man called out. "They want us to stop haying so they can show us pictures?" There was such a tone of bewilderment in his voice that Gareth smiled and others laughed aloud. "They're so smart they're dumb." It was a remark often said about the strangers.

"I'd like to see what their world looks like," another said, a little wistfully.

"So would I. But not now—we don't have the time."

"What if they make us go?"

"They'll have to knock us out to carry us in."

"There aren't enough of them to do that today."

Slowly, quietly, people resumed working. The rakers tried to gather up the scattered hay as best they could. The children helped, bringing back great armfuls that had blown far downhill. Gareth went back to mowing. A dull ache centered in her shoulder muscles that were unused to this type of work. The ache seemed to grow deeper when she thought about the degree of disregard that allowed the strangers to fly above a busy field and order people to forget their work, to come look at pictures—or, instead of disregard, was it arrogance?

CHAPTER
22

LIKE CHILDREN, THE SILVER-SUITS WERE BACK IN THE MORN-ing, insisting on having their way. Airtrucks flew over the hayfields, amplifiers blaring. Apparently a villager had explained the problem: the message had changed. The pictures would be shown in the tent after the workday was over. The amplifiers did not ask but ordered them to be there.

That night at dusk Gareth and her neighbors walked across the fields. The children ran ahead, playing tag, their excited voices echoing the seabirds. A distant storm had raised the surf; the crash and hiss of breakers could be heard far inland. Kite lizards glided high overhead, catching the last rays of the sun on their wings.

Shadowed by the hills behind it, the tent glowed with inner light like a huge phosphorescent puffball. Pole lights stood around its rim; airtrucks gleamed beneath them. As the group from the compound grew closer, they could see villagers crossing the green. There was a party mood about the place.

Most of the people were already in the tent. They sat in clusters on the floor or stood warily facing a large white panel at one end of the oval. Strangers in silver suits strolled along the edges of the crowd, knob-headed in their helmets. It was the first time Paul, Margo, and others had been to the village since the sickness. As they entered, friends waved and called greetings and invitations to join them.

Gareth had never seen everyone crowded into so small a space. The air was close and smelled of well-worn leather, woodsmoke, hay sweat, and faint traces of barnyard boots. She inhaled and decided to remain near the door.

"Is everybody here now? Can we begin?" The translator voice boomed from a nearby speaker. People jumped, and there was nervous laughter. Gareth looked around, trying to see who was talking, and decided it must be the person standing beside the white panel, but it was hard to be sure because of the glare on his helmet. She wondered if Lee Hamlin or her friends were here.

"Where are the pictures?" A child's voice carried above the crowd murmur. "I don't see any pictures—just that big white board. Are they going to draw on it with charcoal?"

"Please? May I have your attention?" The person by the panel raised his arms and waved. "Up here, please." He waited for everyone to settle down. "The pictures you're going to see move and have sound. For those of you who may have seen the screens in our airtrucks, that won't come as anything new. For the rest of you there is no magic involved, nothing to be afraid of. It's simply one of the many benefits of civilization. To make you feel more at ease, we'll start by showing you a few local people and scenes. If you will sit down and watch the screen—"

The lighting dimmed to half its brightness, and people looked around, uneasy. Streaks of blurry color flashed inside the white panel—Gareth thought it looked like grass and sky—and then suddenly she saw herself. She stood atop a mound, looking down and talking. Faces turned in her direction. People pointed, assuring each other she was there. Several children ran to the screen and touched it, trying to catch the stalks of grass waving in the wind, trying to touch her legs. There was more nervous laughter. A flash of light and she was gone, replaced by an aerial view of the cube as it had been before the strangers came. The laughter died. Another flash and there were the village women surf fishing. The salt pans gleamed like snow in the sun. There was Paul, and the compound, then people from the village. The pictures changed so quickly there wasn't time to study them.

The tent was in an uproar. After the initial shock each familiar face or scene was greeted with cries of recognition. Gareth, having seen pictures on the airtruck screens, wasn't surprised by these, but she was awed by understanding what Lee Hamlin and her friends meant by "taking pictures"—it was capturing a moment in time, images from the past. They could make their own dreams.

"Quiet, please!"

The panel went white again, the lights brightened, and the speaker's volume lowered to a comfortable level.

"As you know by now, your ancestors came from Earth—the planet we come from—you are descendants of a colony founded here approximately five hundred years ago. At that time the people here lived very differently than you do now. Our studies suggest that Xilan was first used as a research outpost—which accounts for the MMT and the ruins you call the compound—but that within a few years a civilian population was brought here. . . ."

He paused, as if unsure what to say next, and then he changed the subject. Or at least Gareth thought he did; she wasn't sure what he was trying to tell them.

"The tapes you're going to see—the next pictures—are documentaries selected from our ship's library. They were prepared as educational viewing for children on Earth's colonies. Like yourselves, many of our colonials have never seen the Old World. You are not unique in that respect.

"We anticipate, however, considering your—uh—lack of background, that you will be puzzled by much of what you see. We ask that you save your questions and comments until you've seen all the—uh—pictures.

"Actually, what we want you to do as you watch is to ask yourself if you would like to live in a place like the ones we're going to show you, away from all this hard work, this total vulnerability you experience here. Imagine yourself living in the ease and comfort Earth provides for her people. Now, to give you some perspective—" The lights dimmed again.

Another picture, a green-and-white ball on a field of black. Two tiny spheres appeared suddenly to circle the larger one and disappear behind it.

"This is Xilan and her moons as we see it from our ship. You live approximately here." A pinprick of light flashed in the upper left center of the ball. "And this is our ship, the cruiser *Kekule*."

There was silence in the tent as a metallic form moved across the screen, a totally alien thing, brutal in its simplicity. The speaker's outstretched arm was a silhouette pointing to a golden dot against the surface of the thing. "That tiny speck is one of our maintenance people—which will give you some idea of a starship's size."

This perspective, this altering of perception, was too abrupt for comprehension or acceptance.

"You say that's a man on that thing?" Gareth recognized Luther's voice but couldn't see where he was sitting.

"That is correct. Please don't interrupt."

"That *ship* looks like a big ugly coal cinder to me," said Luther. "And that thing on it is a bug looking for a home. Are you trying to trick us?" There were murmurs of agreement.

The speaker did not answer. The image of the ship remained on screen. Along the edges of the tent the helmeted visitors moved together through the crowd to sit next to Luther. It was so quiet Gareth could hear the surf and seabirds crying in the night.

"We recognize your ignorance," the speaker said. "These pictures are an effort to alleviate that condition. If you all would simply watch and listen quietly—repeat quietly—perhaps that could be accomplished in some small way. We will try to be tolerant."

Gareth shivered, angry and afraid and suddenly sure that these were the same group of strangers who had come to the compound after Lee Hamlin left, the ones who had asked all the intimate questions and seemed so cold. If they lived inside that great ugly ship, if they could tolerate something that inhuman —what sort of people were they?

In the too-quiet tent they showed pictures of Earth and her manufactured satellite worlds. The images changed so quickly, the translator talked so much, that Gareth could understand little of what she saw and heard. It was all too foreign, too unrelated to anything familiar.

Strange buildings covered everything, like a crop too thickly sown and never thinned. Pastel cubicles piled in geometric jumbles; twisted trees grew out of stone tubs; things she guessed were machines roamed at will. Everything, every place, was floored with stone. She saw no open country, no hills or grass or forests, nothing wild. Only buildings and people, more people than she could comprehend, and they all seemed to be playing. The sky was blue instead of green, and she guessed the weather was warm; the people wore scant clothing. There was a sameness about their faces that reminded her of herd animals, a placidness she found disturbing. Every now and then one of them would look out of the picture at the audience and smile. All had perfect teeth and no lines in their faces.

This was the world, these were the people the man in the diary had longed for?

An hour passed, and her eyes hurt. She felt a headache coming on and knew it was from eyestrain. Of the people around her, three were sound asleep, leaning against their companions, snoring. Others sat with eyelids drooping, or they stifled great yawns. She yawned in sympathy, and her eyes teared. They'd all been up since dawn, worked hard all day, and would be up at dawn tomorrow.

A man holding a sleeping child got up and left the tent. People whispered. Several women left with sleep-befuddled youngsters in tow. As if reassured by these examples of normal behavior, some of the older people stood and stretched, stiff from sitting on the floor, then cautiously picked their way through the crowd to the door.

"Don't you want to see more, Everett?" a man called as his friend passed.

The walker dismissed the screen with a wave. "I've seen enough. It's boring and it hurts my eyes. I'm going home to bed." He went out into the night. Others followed.

Gareth considered the walk home and the haying tomorrow and wondered if Paul and the others were ready to go. These pictures might be wonderful if you understood them. If you didn't, they were as soporific as the old instruction books.

As more of the audience began to leave, silver-suits hurried to the doors and tried to turn the defectors back. The villagers simply walked around them.

The translator stopped talking. A picture of a spoked wheel with lights in it, like an odd lantern, remained on the panel. The wheel rotated slowly against its black background.

"I don't believe this!" The silver-suited person stepped up beside the screen again. "I don't believe this!" he repeated. "We show you Earth—civilization at the most advanced state—and you fall asleep! What's wrong with you people? Can't you understand anything? Are you that stupid?"

Gareth heard the anger and contempt the translating machine omitted. She forgot about being sleepy.

"We understand that you are rude, insensitive, and arrogant," she called out as she stood up. "You are uninvited guests. You have imposed yourselves on us, made us sick, disturbed our lives, taken up our time, subjected us to indignities both physical and mental—and now you seem to feel we should be grateful for your rudeness. What's wrong with *you*?"

"Well said!" Paul added his support as he rose.

"Tell 'em, Gareth," Ula urged. "Nasty little bothers."

"Now don't start trouble," Luther pleaded. "Don't make them mad. If they want to show us more pictures that prove how smart they are, we'll watch. It's not much to ask. They made me well."

"You watch," Gareth said. "I'm going home."

There was a bustle of activity as people rose to follow her.

"Wait!" The speakers barked. "You can't go yet! You've got to understand! Whether you like it or not, this colony is doomed." He was talking rapidly, trying to say all he could before they left. "We believe ten thousand people settled here. There are fourteen hundred and thirty-seven of you now. A tenth of you suffer from chronic disease. Your life expectancy is one-third what it should be. We project that within two hundred years there will be so few of you that even this primitive existence you now maintain will be impossible. Soon after that will come a time when there will be one last survivor left on Xilan. But you can escape. You can come with us, come to a place where you can live a better, easier life. We want you to return to the world of your ancestors. We want to take you home."

"Go with them?" They asked the question of each other to verify their understanding. "That's what he said?"

"To that crowded place?"

"We never came from *there*. Look at them. They're not like us at all. Short, squat little things."

"Leave our homes, crops—everything?"

"We'd have to."

"Don't be silly—who'd take care of the animals?"

"He said in two hundred years we'd all be dead if we didn't go with them."

"We'll be dead anyhow. So will he."

Gareth heard all this and more. She turned and looked back at this creature who had just predicted their doom. Everything these little people touched they spoiled. Their very arrival had brought sickness; now they were casting doubt on the far future. They weren't builders; they were destroyers.

"Don't react emotionally," the speaker advised. "Think about it. It's a very generous offer, I assure you."

The tent was empty in two minutes, as if people couldn't flee fast enough from this promise of salvation. Some stood around outside, talking in small groups and watching the silver-suits pack up their things and leave. Gareth was one of the last people out. Paul and the others were waiting for her.

"You go on," she said. "I want to check something out in the records room."

"Tonight?" asked Paul. "Can't it wait?"

"You want to see if it's true?" said Margo. "It is. In essence anyway. You know that. We all know that." She patted Gareth's arm to comfort her. "Might as well come home and go to bed. You've got a hard day tomorrow."

"I'll be along later. Don't close the gate." Gareth left them and almost ran across the green.

Clouds of insects buzzed the pole lights, circling frantically, knocking each other aside in their frenzy to worship these small suns. The sight of the bugs irritated her, as if they were in some way traitors, disloyal to their own way of life.

Dodging the people who called out to her, she hurried down the street, into the comforting darkness at the far end of the village where the meetinghouse stood atop a knoll. Taking the lantern from its niche beside the door, she turned it on and went inside. The room was still and smelled of dry stone and ashes on the hearth. Black bench shadows changed angles on the floor as her lantern passed down the center aisle. In the records room at the rear of the hall, she lit a second lantern and by their joint dimness mixed up ink and sat down to calculate the truth of what the strangers said.

The record books were old and heavy. Each had to be unwrapped from its protective oilskin, then rewrapped and tied. The population first recorded two hundred and eighty years before had been eighteen hundred and nine. A hundred years later it was down to sixteen hundred and twenty-one. Fifty years after that the total was fifteen hundred and eighteen. And so it went, down to the present. There was no one reason she could find, or even guess at, for the declining birthrate. The cause of death most often listed was "pneumonia," at an average age of forty-three for adults, six months for infants.

She started to calculate how many years it would take at this rate for there to be no one left on Xilan, then stopped. She didn't want to know.

As Margo said, the figures told her nothing she hadn't known before—that everyone hadn't known before. But it was unspoken, accepted as the way things were—and nothing could be done about it. Until now.

She closed the books and put them back onto their shelves, carefully, precisely, and in her mind pictured the alternative offered by the Builders. Imagine yourself on Earth, they said, and she imagined the endless buildings, the artificial trees and flowers, the crowds of people—all staring at her as these visitors did because she was taller than they.

After seeing the pictures, she could understand why Earth people would want to come to Xilan, but she could not understand why anyone would want to go to Earth. The promise of a longer life? At that thought she smiled to herself; it was like the old family joke: "You don't live longer. It just seems that way." Still, what if people decided they wanted to go? They might, once they thought over that promise—especially people like Luther and the others who were being cured of illnesses she couldn't even diagnose. And Xilan children born on Earth would never miss their own world.

To go would mean never seeing her home again. But then if she'd died out there by the water hole on the plains— She paused in her thinking, realizing she was equating *going away* with death.

But was that fair, or was it ignorance on her part, as the silver-suit had said? To leave her home, to leave her house and all its memories behind . . . to *escape the responsibility that house represented.* She considered that. If they went with the Builders, she'd never again have to watch someone suffer because she was helpless to stop it, never have to feel responsible for pain, or train someone to help her and take her place if she should die early, or make an incision and pray she wasn't cutting something vital, or deliver another delicate baby without getting sick with fear that she might damage both mother and child. Just imagining such freedom made her feel slightly giddy. And all she had to pay for such freedom was all she was.

She turned shut the desk lantern and went back outside. The lights were off down by the tent. The airtrucks were gone. The night was restored to its natural state, and the stars could be seen again. A few windows glowed with lamplight, but most were dark.

From the barns came the thumps of a blue strider kicking its stable wall and bleating. Striders often had bad dreams. They remembered their life before capture. As she listened, Gareth wondered if animals were as simple as people thought they were. Perhaps, if she was taken to Earth, she would kick the walls and cry.

CHAPTER
23

"WESLEY HALL WOULD LIKE TO STAY." TAI WAS SITTING ON Lee's bed, leaning back against the wall. "He likes the place. He says if we stayed, with time and study he could make life better for the people here." She slid another turquoise onto the necklace she was stringing, tied a square anchoring knot, and held the string up to inspect it.

"And if he could stay, would you?" Lee asked. She was stretched out on the floor, hands clasped behind her head.

"Oh, sure. Earth would be an empty place without him."

Lee nodded as if she had assumed as much. "They won't allow it, you know. Your contracts forbid it."

"I'm counting on that." Tai smiled down at her friend. "Besides, I think he wants to stay as penance, to expiate his sins in case some of the other worlds we've worked on turn out to be like Xilan."

"It's not a comforting thought."

"Do you believe it?"

Lee waited to answer until Tai stopped buffing a blue nugget; its roughness had displeased her. "I don't know. The people here survived with no help at all. If their original technology hadn't failed—if ships had come back with support—maybe . . ."

"Maybe," Tai conceded, "but I doubt there's any way we can filter all the metals out. Not to acceptable tolerance. Anything grown in this soil, every drop of water, every animal that's edible—I think now that's what made me witchy when we landed. I could feel it all around me. The longer we stay, the less sensitive I am to it."

"And you'd stay here with Wes? Believing that?"

"Yes. Wesley Hall is home."

They were quiet for a time, each lost in her own thoughts, comfortable together.

"Sometimes lately I've thought I'd like a home." Lee spoke again. "Something more than an officer's suite on a ship endlessly moving through time. Do you remember the *Flying Dutchman*?"

Tai shook her head.

"There's an ancient myth on Earth about a ship called the *Flying Dutchman*. Its captain is immortal—doomed to sail forever, to outlive everyone he meets, everyone he loves. One gets so tired of saying good-bye and knowing you'll never meet again. I said good-bye when I left home and went to school on Earth. And when school was over, I said good-bye to Earth. I went home again to tell them I was going into space. . . . We cried. . . . In my memory my parents are still young. I'm older now than they were then. They never traveled much."

Tai went on stringing her necklace. A single tear slid down her cheek. She didn't brush it away, afraid of making her friend self-conscious. After a moment Lee continued.

"On my first voyage I fell in love. We were both nineteen. When the trip was over, he took a job on Earth and I went on to Tanin. When we met again, he was fifty-four. Three years had passed for me. We looked at each other, and we began to cry. I cried for two weeks . . . but then I understood. I never made that mistake again. I've been very careful not to care too much."

"You and the Flying Dutchman?" Tai asked carefully.

"We're all Flying Dutchmen. Everyone who goes to space."

"And isn't it wonderful?" said Tai. "Don't feel sorry for yourself. We chose the life we wanted. It's enabled us to see a million things most people never get to, to live well and be healthy, to learn all we can in the field we chose. If we chose to be lonely too, that's our fault, no one else's. Sometimes I look at you and Singh, and I'd like to shake you both. You're perverse!"

"We're not! We're professionals. We're disciplined."

Tai looked down at Lee and shook her head. "Yes. You are that, too. And both of you are letting time slip by. . . ."

The door opened and Wes and Major Singh came in, smelling of soap and the showers. "Stevens is down here," Wes announced in greeting. "We saw him on the courts—he came in this evening."

"He's a lousy squash player," Singh added, sitting on the workbench. "Even with his gofers. They're here, too. And the sociologists."

"What's he doing on the surface?" Tai asked.

"He has—I quote his aide—devised an educational program for the colonists that will minimize their departure fears and maximize anticipation to join civilization at a minimum cost to the corporation." Wes added, "The fool."

"Can you imagine a girl like Gareth," said the major, "who thinks nothing of walking a hundred miles through the woods, shut into a project with a quarter-mile-square park? She'd die . . . she'd . . ." He caught himself before he slipped into emotion. "I don't think she'd like it very much."

"Paul thought we sounded like prisoners, let out of our cages only when we came to a new world," Wesley Hall remembered. "He kept saying, 'It must be hard to live that way,' and it is. I envy them—"

"Oh, Wes, be practical," Lee said. "They might be able to adjust to us in time—the young ones especially—but we can't survive here. Not without our total support system. For all your talk of a natural life, you couldn't live as they do. It's very easy to go up in physical comforts, but terrible to come down."

"I could learn," he insisted.

"Probably. If you lived through the first month. But could you stand watching our last shuttle leave?"

"It's out of the question," Singh said quietly. "I'd get you on the shuttle, by force if I had to. So don't waste time discussing or even thinking about staying here."

"Well, that settles that," Tai said a bit too quickly. "Now tell us why Stevens came down himself instead of sending someone else."

"Nathan told him half the R and D staff would resign in protest if the colonists were forcibly removed," said Singh. "If they resigned, the corporation could scrap the next three projects or be forced to delay while they hired and trained new people. Stevens could see time and money going down the tubes and the reason for the loss blamed on him. He'd never get another job, let alone promoted."

"Where did Nathan get the idea so many would resign?" asked Tai.

"I told him they would." Singh's teeth gleamed as he grinned.

"He believed you?"

"Either that or he thought the threat made as good a bluff as I did. Stevens is flying over to the village tomorrow."

"What if we find Xilan can't be safely used as a colony—ever?" Lee asked. "What's the point of trying to move the people then?"

"Oh, then, you see, it becomes a humanitarian rescue mission with Stevens in charge and getting glory," Wes explained. "Think how beautiful Gareth and Paul and the others look on screen. With the right promotion, the right propaganda, the corporation can not only reassure potential future colonists, but gain a lot of free publicity as a group who cares about people. It could be made quite touching. A sales plus, Stevens called it."

An explosive slam brought Lee abruptly to her feet. Major Singh had hit the table with his fist. There was a crack all the way across the table's surface.

"Sorry," he apologized as he rubbed a bloody knuckle. "I got a little upset. I'm going to have to stay away from you three. You make me think of things I don't want to know. I'm sorry," he said again and went out.

"You see," Tai said after a moment, "there are limits to discipline."

Three nights later, Gareth wrote in her journal:

I don't know which is worse, their arrogance or their persistence. I think I prefer the former; it's far less disruptive. Ever since we saw their pictures, we've been plagued by silver-suits and their endless efforts to convince us to leave Xilan. They follow us everywhere —to the fields, the barns, the kitchen. We have to work around them, in spite of them. They're always underfoot. It's impossible to hold a normal conversation in their presence. If they're not talking, their translators are. They've taken all the fun out of haying. Out of everything, in fact.

They've placed what they call teaching screens in various houses in the village—and one here in Margo's dome. The screens show endless pictures of their world while a translator explains them. Margo plugged the speaker with mud. She couldn't stand the noise. At night she throws a rug across the screen. Light flashes as the pictures change, and it's irritating.

To help convince us of the benefits of their world, they repaired the teeth of all who would allow them to—well and without pain! I was very impressed. They tested people's vision and gave those with less than good eyesight what they called corrective lenses. Margo was so happy to see clearly again that she cried. Paul says he's never seen so well, even as a child. He acts ten years younger now that he's no longer afraid of falling. I never knew he had that fear.

There's so much I don't know, so much I'd like to learn. If I went with them, perhaps they could teach me—but then where would I use the knowledge? Machines are the medics in their world.

For all their talk, they don't explain what we would do in their world, how we'd pass the days. They talk of "education" and "rehabilitation," but the talk is vague, and when asked for specifics they say, "We'll worry about that later"—as though we were a problem they hadn't thoroughly thought through.

Paul asked why, if Xilan was so bad for people, they planned to bring more people here, and their answer was that if they did that, they would change what was wrong with the world—which seems illogical as well as boastful.

C H A P T E R
24

"GOOD NIGHT, GARETH," SOMEONE CALLED, AND OTHERS echoed good night. She turned and waved to the group following the loaded wagons. The setting sun glared in her eyes, and she couldn't tell who called, so she put down her scythe and waved with both arms for good measure. The windrows cast blue shadows, supper smoke rose from chimneys, the air smelled of hay and sea. Even though she was tired, the sight contented her. No silver-suits had come today, and without them the work went much faster. The hill field had been cut and raked and the bottom field hauled in. If the weather held, they'd be finished in two days.

She turned and started home, arms wrapped around the scythe handle balanced on her shoulders, weaving slightly from exhaustion as she trudged up the road through the trees. Uri and the others walked ahead, their voices rousing birds already gone to roost.

She hoped no one got sun-sick tonight as they had the night before. She didn't welcome the idea of being wakened the second night in a row to hurry over to the village. In the house she hung the scythe in the toolroom and went to the dispensary to ready her medical kit and make sure she had a lantern ready, before going up to bathe.

The water from the hearth reservoir was cold. She shivered as she bathed in the room Major Singh had called "primitive but ingenious." She found when she was tired that she thought about them more; she was beginning to resent their almost total occupation of her mind. With a stiff brush she cleaned her nails; her hands felt bruised from the weight of the scythe, and she had two new blisters.

"Gareth? Supper's ready," Margo called from the front hall hallway.

"Two minutes." She toweled with a soft chamois-like cloth made from the skins of a small burrowing animal, donned a brown shift of the same material, belted it with a wide plaited belt Uri had made for her, birthdays ago, and combed her hair. "Coming!" she called and went into her bedroom, to find Margo holding the work clothes Gareth had flung across a chair.

"Those can walk by themselves," Gareth said quickly and apologetically.

"I noticed," was the older woman's reply. "I'll take them home to soak overnight. I'm going to boil wash in the morning."

"You've got clothes enough to do." Gareth tried to retrieve the garments, but Margo evaded the grab. "It's so dusty in the fields—the pants can go another day."

"You're not a villager," said Margo. "You mustn't dress like one. And don't argue with me. I'm old and deserve respect."

"By virtue of your age?"

"By the age of my virtue," Margo said, and they laughed, pleased with this nonsense and with each other. "Speaking of age, I stewed a venerable hen most of the afternoon. Along with my vegetables, Paul's added dumplings. I can hardly stir the pot, the gravy's gotten so thick."

"Let's hurry before it solidifies," said Gareth. "I'm about to eat my arm."

Because of the cold bath and hunger, the air outside felt cold and the grass that brushed her bare legs made her shiver. Across the compound, near the barn, she saw Uri carrying a lantern, going to feed the animals before he sat down to eat. The first stars were out. The glow of the dome was visible now in the dusk.

As soon as he saw them come in the door, Paul began ladling stew into bowls and cut chunks off the crusty bread. Their hunger limited talk in the early part of the meal to such basics as "Delicious," "Have another piece of bread?" and "Please pass the wine." By the time civilized conversation evolved, the stewpot was empty, the bone dish full, and Gareth was having a hard time keeping her eyes open.

"Was that lightning?" Paul interrupted himself in the middle of a sentence. "I don't remember clouds." Just then what appeared to be a ball of light struck the dome overhead, suffused through its opacity, and flashed away. From the distance came the sound of an approaching airtruck. They looked at one another; there went the quiet evening.

"Perhaps if we sit quietly, they'll think we've gone to bed," Margo suggested.

"You stay here. I'll go see," Gareth volunteered, and received no argument.

The aircraft came in over the woods, revolving lights on its belly sweeping the blowing treetops and sending cones of brightness fanning over the compound. People came out to look, some carrying their dinner plates. "Just what we need—more visitors," she heard Uri grumble to his wife. "It's not enough they waste our days. Now they come at night." There was the sound of closing doors, and Gareth stood alone.

The craft eased itself into the space in front of her door. She sighed. The lemonberry bushes hadn't recovered from their last beating by jet wash. The motors stopped. Cabin lights went on, landing lights went off, and the hatch hissed open.

"Lord, it's dark!" she heard Tai say. "I'd forgotten how dark it got out here."

"But *smell*," said Wesley Hall. "Just smell—it's wonderful." Footsteps rang on the metal ramp.

"Do you think they're all in bed?" That was Lee Hamlin's voice.

"It's too early," was Major Singh's opinion. "Watch your eyes now—I'm putting on the field lights." The sudden glare was so painful that Gareth cried out.

"Gareth?" questioned the major, and the light swung away.

They greeted her as if she were a long-lost friend.

"We're not supposed to be here," Tai confided. "We had to sneak away. Management doesn't want us to be an adverse influence, quote-unquote, in their campaign to convince you to come with us. As it is, our careers are probably casualties of Xilan."

"We brought back your books." Lee spoke quickly, as if to stop Tai from saying too much. "And we wanted to talk to you while we still had the chance."

In that last phrase Gareth saw a gleam of hope, a hint they might soon be gone. The idea cheered her so that she relaxed a bit. "I'll help you carry in the books. We can stack them in the hall—" She couldn't wait to know. "Is your ship leaving soon? Leaving Xilan?"

The four exchanged glances.

"You sound as if you'd be glad to see us go," Lee said.

Gareth didn't want to lie, but neither did she want to be rude. She smiled and bent to lift a stack of books from the ramp and carried them inside. After hesitating, her visitors began to help. Some of the books appeared to have been roughly handled; pages protruded at odd angles; covers were falling off. Others had cracks in their spines from end to end as if they'd been opened and forced flat. She fingered one of the worst damaged.

"That happened during copying," Lee said. "I'm sorry."

"I can fix it," Gareth said. "I'm glad to get them back."

"You didn't think you would?"

"I was beginning to doubt it."

"Why?"

"It's a matter of regard," said Gareth. "You people say everything we have is 'primitive' and dismiss its worth."

"That's not true," said the major, overhearing this conversation. "People tried to steal these books as collector's items. They're very valuable. That's why we brought them back, to protect them. And because we four had promised."

"I'm grateful," Gareth said, but she wasn't sure for what. "Are you leaving Xilan soon?" she asked, returning to her most important question.

"They haven't set a date yet, but they will soon, yes." Lee glanced around the dimly lit hallway and looked toward the open door, as if she felt uncomfortable inside. "Are you coming with us?"

"No."

"None of you?"

"Not that I know of."

"I'm glad," the woman said.

"You didn't come here to try to talk us into it?" Gareth asked as she followed them outside.

"No." Lee sat down on the hatch and the others followed her lead. Gareth considered this act of settling down and wondered what was coming. "There's something we must tell you. It may make you as angry as our entering the MMT, but if you ever go back north again—"

"You opened the mound!" Gareth guessed and felt slightly sick to her stomach.

"We opened seven of them," Tai said and paused, as if waiting for Gareth's response, but there was nothing to say. The thing was done. It probably looked like the cube now, raw and ugly.

"I had it graded and resodded," Major Singh said then. "Considering what it is, it seemed the proper thing to do. It won't upset you to see it—not after a rain or two, to make the grass grow."

"We discovered a number of things we thought you should know." Lee Hamlin went on. "Earth's colony—your ancestors —was not the first on Xilan. There are ruins of four others scattered over the planet. All are different. We don't know how long the one you found lasted, but there is evidence some of the creatures still survived when humans first reached Xilan."

"They weren't human?"

"No. They were . . . sentients. There are the ruins of a city about ten miles due north." She shrugged. "We don't know what they were—and we've seen their bodies. What's left of them. Most are dust. But we found several well enough preserved to tell how they died—among other things. Two had been burned by lasers, three killed by copper slugs."

Gareth was trying to understand all this. "You mean *my* people shot them?"

"It would appear so . . . long ago."

"On purpose?"

"I don't know." Lee shook her head. "If you can't communicate—intelligence is hard to recognize in the absence of technology or tools—"

"Or with it," Wesley Hall interjected.

"They had fur," Lee continued. "They needed no clothing. And to humans, fur is automatically translated as 'animal.' They were short, stocky creatures, bipeds, not native to the planet."

"People killed them off?" Gareth was still frowning.

"People killed a few. We suspect the prime cause of death was incompatibility with the environment."

It took Gareth a little while to translate some of this in her mind. To describe a tragedy, the woman was using words laundered of all feeling. Why? Was it her way, their way, habit acquired by always viewing things from the air, distant and without feeling?

"The burial capsules were lying out of place, as if not enough people were left to do it properly," Lee was saying, "but of particular interest is how the aliens' physique changed over the years. The bodies in the last few mounds are different from the first—elongated, the bones more delicate—"

"You're telling me the same thing happened to them that has and will happen to us." Gareth's voice was nearly a whisper. "Aren't you?"

"There might be a parallel, yes."

"You said there were other ruins. Did you dig those up, too?"

"We won't have time . . ." Lee hesitated. "Ruins of ancient

colonies aren't all that rare in our experience." She glanced at her friends as if they would verify that statement. They nodded rather glumly. They looked different, Gareth thought, since the first time she'd seen them. More finely drawn, as if they were still recovering, or maybe suffering from some grief.

"They appeared more suited to this world than any human would be," Wesley Hall said, staring off into space. He appeared to be talking to himself.

"The sociologists—the silver-suits—will be here tomorrow or the next day to tell you that we will soon leave, that your people have only a few days to decide if they want to come with us. If the decision is no, it will be a long time before another Earth ship orbits Xilan. If ever."

"You won't bring more people here?"

"I sincerely doubt it."

"That's good news!"

They laughed as if surprised by her response, and then, sobering, Tai asked. "Are you sure you understand the situation? You'll be happier on this world—but you'll be alone out here."

"But we always were," said Gareth, and kept herself from adding, We liked it better that way. "You want to know if I understand that in time there will be no more people here? Yes. We've always assumed that. Is that what you came to tell me? To make sure I understood?" It seemed callous of them, from her point of view.

"Partly. We thought *you* did." Lee hesitated. "Actually, we came to apologize for our trespassing, for what must seem to be insensitivity. We're not all like that, you know." She gestured vaguely toward the books. "Most of us are like the people who wrote those books—or we would be under similar circumstances. I don't know why we've changed. . . ."

"Because your world is dead," Gareth said quickly, and then regretted it; it sounded rude, but it was true. "There's nothing there but people and machines. Not that we could see. . . . I know you live the way you think people ought to live. And you think the way you look is correct—and that we're primitive and not worth much. Perhaps we aren't to you. We couldn't live the way you do. We couldn't stand being shut up like that." She hesitated, not sure how to make them understand what she felt. "The thought of going to your world is as frightening to us as the thought of being forced to stay here is frightening to you."

Major Singh shifted uncomfortably, and Wesley Hall swallowed as if his throat were dry.

"Maybe our being here is a mistake," Gareth continued, "so far as you're concerned. Maybe we won't progress the way you think we should. Maybe I will die at the same age my parents did while you live twice as long or longer. But I wouldn't trade my life for yours, my time here for your world. And in a way I will live as long as you, for you'll remember me." She smiled then to herself, pleased by a thought. "And when I have a child I will tell it about you, and it will tell its child, and so on. So you'll be remembered, too."

She looked into their faces and for a time searched them, trying to find a way across the barrier of culture and time. But there was no way. They left shortly afterward, saying they'd be back.

"Who was that?" Paul asked when she returned to the table.

"Lee Hamlin and the other three."

"What did they want?"

"To be forgiven."

CHAPTER
25

THE SILVER-SUITS WERE BACK IN THE MORNING AS LEE HAMLIN
had said they would be. They went from compound to hayfield to
village, making their final offer. Nothing was said about the
mounds or other alien ruins, but it seemed to Gareth that they'd
lost interest, as if whatever their original motives had been in
wanting people off Xilan, now they no longer cared. They left at
noontime and took with them their tent and their equipment.

"There goes our new woodshed," Luther grumbled as the
airtrucks took off.

"Wouldn't have lasted anyway," another man consoled him.
"It's not as if it were built of stone. It was made of skin and air."

"It was fireproof," Luther said. "I know—I tried to burn it."

"Do you think we'll see any of them again?" a boy asked rather
wistfully. "They didn't say good-bye."

"They never said hello," Ula reminded them. "They just
walked in as if they owned things. Us included."

Work in the field had hardly resumed when more airtrucks
arrived, not at the village this time but on the cliff beneath the
cube. They unloaded machines that promptly stirred up so much
dust no one could see what they were doing.

"Maybe they're tearing it down and taking it with them?"
someone suggested, but that didn't seem logical—something
that big. One airtruck took off and disappeared in the distance. It
returned in late afternoon. Slung beneath it on a hoist were
several large silk trees, their roots net-wrapped. The craft passed
over the hayfield, slowed and hovered over the clifftop.

It was hard to see against the afternoon sun, but Gareth thought she saw the trees being eased down, one by one, as if they were being planted, and she wondered at that. She would have liked to go to investigate, but there was no time. They still had more than half the field to load and haul in. If they worked until dusk tonight, they might finish the job by tomorrow. Besides, she thought, who wanted to see the cube the way it was now.

Three days passed before curiosity took her up there. The sun had already set, and in the near dusk the place looked as it had before its desecration. The building beneath the cube had been reburied, the ground contoured and smoothed. Fallen trees had been trimmed to logs and neatly stacked in a pile. New trees had been planted. Shrubs grew where none had before and, most surprising of all, sod had been laid in long strips and the grass was green.

She stood and stared, as shocked as she had been the last time she was here. The repair was as awesome to her as the destruction had been. That people could be capable of doing things like this—and with such speed and ease—perhaps they *could* rearrange an entire world to suit their needs and wishes. Her gardener's eye told her it would be several years before the place looked healed, but then it would be parklike, prettier than before—if without its spirit.

To the east of the building, in a rocky hollow, she came upon a tiny pool and fountain, new and almost hidden by trees. One side of a big gray boulder had been slabbed away and words cut into the rock:

MITCHELL OBSERVATORY, CIRCA 4000.

EXCAVATED AND REBURIED FOR PRESERVATION,

JULY 4509.

LANDSCAPING BY A. K. SINGH, MAJOR, TFSF,

FOR GARETH MITCHELL AND HER CHILDREN

She sat down on her haunches and puzzled the words out of

the strange block script. The job looked as if it had been done hastily; the cutting tool had slipped here and there. She traced a mar with her fingertip; the cut felt smooth and glassy.

Seabirds cried warning. The dark cube looming above her began to turn slowly. She rose, smiling, brushed off her hands, and looked to see what star it might be watching. She could see at least a dozen in the darkening sky. All looked the same to her. The cube stopped. And then far out over the sea flew an object high enough to catch the last rays of the sun—a bright oblong that shrank into a star and was gone.

The boy was right; they weren't going to say good-bye, but then "good-bye" was hardly adequate.

She walked slowly down the path to the beach, remembering the last time she'd gone home this way. The beach still looked the same. So did the valley. Nothing had really changed. They had come and gone. That was all, and four of them would be remembered. Like the land around the cube, it might take several years before life got back to normal. But everything would be as it had been. Of course it would. Of course it would.

About the Author

H. M. HOOVER is one of America's leading writers of science fiction for young people. She is the author of *The Delikon*, *The Rains of Eridan*, *The Lost Star*, *Return to Earth*, and *This Time of Darkness*, all published by Viking.

Ms. Hoover lives near Washington, D. C., where she pursues her interests in natural history, archaeology, and history, as well as writing. She is now at work on a new novel.